Praise for
GOLD DUST

"Lynch captures the thrill of the game."
—ALA *Booklist* (boxed review)

"Lynch's provocative novel tells a piece of
[Boston's] history and the more intimate story
of a transforming friendship."
—*The Horn Book* (starred review)

"[Richard and Napoleon's] tenuous friendship is one
readers are bound to respect and remember."
—*The Bulletin of the Center for Children's Books*

OTHER BOOKS BY CHRIS LYNCH

SHADOW BOXER

ICEMAN

GYPSY DAVEY

POLITICAL TIMBER

SLOT MACHINE

EXTREME ELVIN

WHITECHURCH

The Blue-Eyed Son Trilogy:
#1 MICK
#2 BLOOD RELATIONS
#3 DOG EAT DOG

CHRIS LYNCH

GOLD DUST

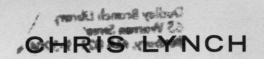 HarperTrophy®
An Imprint of HarperCollins*Publishers*

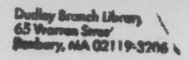

Harper Trophy® is a registered trademark of
HarperCollins Publishers Inc.

Gold Dust
Text copyright © 2000 by Chris Lynch

Library of Congress Cataloging-in-Publication Data
Lynch, Chris.
  Gold dust / Chris Lynch.
    p.   cm.
  Summary: In 1975, twelve-year-old Richard befriends Napoleon, a
Caribbean newcomer to his Catholic school, hoping that Napoleon will
learn to love baseball and the Red Sox, and will win acceptance in the
racially polarized Boston school.
  ISBN 0-06-028174-X — ISBN 0-06-028175-8 (lib. bdg.)
  ISBN 0-06-447201-9 (pbk.)
  [1. Racism—Fiction. 2. Baseball—Fiction. 3. Friendship—Fiction. 4.
Schools—Fiction. 5. Caribbean Americans—Fiction. 6. Boston (Mass.)—
Fiction.] I. Title.
PZ7.L979739 Go   2000   00-024348
[Fic]—dc21   CIP
                                                                      AC

Typography by Alison Donalty
❖
First Harper Trophy edition, 2002

Visit us on the World Wide Web!
www.harperchildrens.com

To my buddy Jacqueline Woodson
extraordinary writer,
friend,
role model.
For reminding me that
good intentions
are not
good enough.

CONTENTS

conversation or something like that, it came back. He did
not do anything that I could tell. He was thinking about it.

So then, the goal is to be like you? That is the key to
the...

GOLD DUST

SHORTCHANGE

Napoleon Charlie Ellis showed up just after Christmas. When he landed here there was almost a foot of snow on the ground. When he took off from Dominica, there probably was not.

That was the first shortchanging he got. The second was that they shoved him back down into seventh grade when he was supposed to be in the eighth. Language problem was what they were talking about. What language did you speak back home in Dominica, I asked him. English, he told me, and told me in some pretty fine English, I must say. So I didn't quite get why they did that. Anyway.

"They announced my name when I came in," he said to me. "So you have the advantage of me."

"Huh?"

"What is your name?"

"It ain't half what your name is."

"Ain't?" Napoleon Charlie Ellis asked me, sounding

very surprised. My ain't never surprised anybody in the past. Mr. Ellis apparently expected Boston, Massachusetts, USA, Hub of the Solar System, Athens of America, to be an Ain't-Free-Zone. It would be my job to enlighten him.

Richard Riley Moncreif, I told him. *Ain't* it purdy? I added. I was loaded with confidence that day, and lots of days before then too. Meeting people, talking to people, mixing . . . I never had any problem with that the way a lot of people do.

Napoleon Charlie Ellis stuck out his hand, right there in the boys' bathroom, and after a small pause I stuck out mine. My hand.

It was an excellent shake, kind of formal, kind of hard, little bit of challenge, little bit squeezy. I had very little experience with the hand-shaking bit since it was never really much of a thing in my circle, and I never figured it to be all that crammed with meaning, the way grown men take it so seriously. But if I wanted to try thinking that there was more to it than a couple of guys trying to show each other how firm their grip was, I might have thought, this feels like the hand of somebody I could like.

But I didn't want to try thinking that. Don't make things more complicated than they should be would be my philosophy if I had one. So.

It was a fairly tough grip to match squeeze for squeeze if it came down to it. That was what I thought mattered about the handshake of Napoleon Charlie Ellis.

He was well known before he knew it, his story circulating through our little population before he did. He was not a full year older than me, despite the being kept back thing, which they could call lots of other things but we recognized as being kept back. I was on the old side of seventh and Napoleon was on the young side of eighth, so we were pretty close anyhow. I'm sure he recognized that and that was one reason we became friends so quickly. And I was a little bit taller too, so he could respect me, even if this was only my first run-through of the seventh grade.

"I do wish you wouldn't do that," he said to me.

"Do what?"

"Making the jokes. About my getting reversed. I don't care for it. I can forget about it when you don't mention it, since there is nobody here who knew me when I was in eighth grade, but when you bring it up, I am reminded. I don't care to be reminded."

Which was, I guess, the third part of the shortchanging of Napoleon Charlie Ellis. All his people were somewhere else.

"I'll stop," I said. Napoleon had a very smart face. Could make me appreciate things I couldn't manage on my own. This could be a good thing or a bad thing, depending on what you wanted out of a guy. Mostly, I was happy enough knowing what I knew, and doing what I did. So this was a thing that we'd have to keep an eye on.

But as long as he had me looking, what did I know

about being removed from my everything? That was for sure something Napoleon had that I didn't. All my people were right here around me, always were and always would be. I had what and who I needed right here. Mine was that kind of neighborhood, that kind of life. "I'm sorry," I said, mostly just to make the thing go away. "I'll stop."

"Yes, you said that," he said.

See there, he could have said, okay, cool, Richard. Great. He could, and obviously did, notice that I felt bad enough to repeat myself. Could have let me off easier then. So what did he do instead? Pointed it *out* to me, that I had repeated. Threw a spotlight on it. Cold spot. And that was the way he did things. Letting a guy off was not his way. Like if I made a mistake with him I had to feel it twice, as if I couldn't really get it the first time. Frankly, I didn't understand why a guy should be that tense.

"Oh right, well I just repeated myself because I know you have that problem with the English and all."

Times like this, a joke at just the right moment can really smooth things . . .

"Where are you going, Napoleon? Come back, wouldja please just . . ."

Did I ask for this? Was I looking for this? Did I go following anybody into the bathroom to spark up a friendship? No, I did not. I was minding my own business, doing just fine, marking off days on the calendar until baseball season started. Next thing I know I'm chasing a guy out of the bathroom to patch things up. Makes no sense. If I ran things, nobody would have names. We would just have batting averages. Then there would be no misunderstandings.

In the meantime, Napoleon Charlie would not get shortchanged by me at least.

"I'm sorry," I said, catching him at the foot of the yellowed marble steps of the school basement. "I didn't mean anything. I swear."

His face remained rigid, only slowly and slightly softening. Then he nodded.

"So, what's your batting average?" I asked.

He let his face freeze again, then headed up the stairs.

"What?" I said, following. "That one wasn't a joke. That was a real question. Jeez, man, you eat a box of nails for breakfast, or *what*?"

HARD
DOWN
THE
MIDDLE

I am not a scientist.

And I'm not a poet or a bishop or a musician or an architect or a statesman or a television repairman.

Lots of things don't make sense to me. The solar system, for one. God. Evolution, the piano and anyone who plays it, and the Red Sox not winning the World Series even one time since 1918.

These things are unexplainable.

Here's another. A city where the people dislike each other so much that the court had to force the different kinds of kids to sit together in school. Where people throw rocks and try to tip over school buses. Where the *mothers* of some students show up on the news at night and they are screaming the most horrible things they can think of at the kids on the buses. And then one of those same mothers comes on the interview to say it's not about hating anybody.

I'm fairly certain in that case that I do not understand

what it is about. I'm not even close. And it hurts my head to try, so I don't.

"You see this?" I say to Butchie, holding my baseball bat high in the air like Thor with his hammer. "I am going to take *this*, and I am going to hit *that* ball, out into *that* patch of bushes in left."

It is that simple. And it is true. I know it and Butchie knows it. It is a beautiful, simple fact.

"Hard. Down the middle, Butch. That's what I want."

"Anybody can hit that, Richard. Big deal."

"No, anybody cannot hit that. You, for example, can't hit that."

"Can."

"Can't. I'm talkin' hard. Crank it up and let it go. You can start throwing me your junk in another week or two. I'm not gonna mess myself up trying to hit live balls two months before anybody even wants to play a real game. But you *can* throw it just as fast as you want. I only want to swing the bat and hit the ball. Hard, and hard. Simple."

I love every bit of it. I love the sound. The sound of the ball approaching, whistling, if it's thrown with the right snap. The sound of my bat whipping around, again, a sort of whistle in there. But above all . . . of course. Above all what I love is the sound of my bat hitting his ball. I can hit it. I can hit any one.

I don't do a lot of bragging. But I do my share. It's just part of the game. A fun part. Anything that adds fun to the game is okay anyway, and doesn't do any harm as long as you're not a jerk about it. So I can talk a little, when the opportunity arises.

It doesn't arise all that often when I'm playing basketball. I'm okay at basketball, but just as okay as a zillion other guys. Or football, at which I am better than basketball, but not better than, say, a billion other guys. Or hockey or skeet shooting or Tae Kwan Do, all of which I have tried and none of which I have embarrassed myself at, but neither have I set the world on fire with.

But I can hit a baseball.

Can throw one too.

But I can *hit* a baseball. I *understand* hitting a baseball.

"Pitchers are always ahead of hitters in the first weeks, Butchie, so it won't prove anything for you to snap a curve past me in February, will it?"

"Might not prove anything, but it'll sure feel good."

Butchie grins. He's got a good, intimidating pitcher's grin, to go with a very stretched-out body and great wingspan that both give him excellent leverage and the appearance of being even faster than he is. He's tough enough too, in that desperate way pitchers need to be.

I stand in there, scratching hard into the frozen dirt of the petrified batter's box with my spikes. Butchie keeps grinning, leans back, and back and back, then comes over the top, and over and over, and finally reaches his perfect release point and lets go of the first pitch of the 1975 baseball season.

It whistles. It is such a beautiful thing, the sound of it, the east-west spin—which I can pick up easily in the superior clarity of winter's air—that I am almost too excited to react properly to the pitch until . . .

I drop to the ground, flopping hard on my back an instant before the ball nails me in the head.

"If you can't stand the heat . . ." Butchie says, blowing warm steaming air through his pitching hand.

Could've told you he was going to do that.

I do love this game.

COMMUNITY

According to Napoleon, his mother chose to send him to St. Colmcille's for the sense of community.

I squinted. "Community," I repeated, in a way that was not a question, exactly, but did communicate confusion.

"Catholic community," he pointed out.

"Catholic," I said. "So you're Catholic? Huh. Go figure."

Napoleon shook his head at me. Already not an unusual reaction. "Yes," he said, "go figure."

I should have been getting used to imports of new types to the school by now. Up until my sixth grade year it was nearly unheard of for anybody to come to this school by any other method besides on foot. Neighborhood school, and all. It was a nice school, comfortable old building, big playground, couple of trees splashed around, Garcia's Superette, which sold everything smaller than a car, right on the corner. But it was probably not unlike loads of other parochial schools all over the place. Same uniforms, same Pledge of Allegiance, same boring subjects, same Jesus. So there was never any reason for folks to go to any great trouble to send their kids across the city any distance to get here.

Until the busing thing. Kids crisscrossing the city to go to *public* schools. In *other* neighborhoods.

Other people's public schools.

And that's when the "community" thing got big. It was all over the papers. People were defending their "community schools" as something sacred. So lots of people bailed out and started sending their kids to Catholic schools. For the community. No matter how far away the community happened to be. I had to wonder if I just didn't know what the C word meant, or if somebody was changing it.

"What time is it, boys?"

"Oh no, please, not this."

"Come on, Manny, what time is it?"

Manny sighed. Glen stared at me very serious, like a teacher. "Can't you talk about anything else?" Glen asked. Glen was about the sharpest guy we had. Knew all kinds of things. Most of which I figure a person doesn't really need to know. "There are lots of other things worth thinking about."

I gave him back the look. "No there ain't."

Manny lifted the top of his flip-top desk and made like he was disappearing into it. Glen just shook his head and returned to reading.

Napoleon Charlie Ellis entered the room and sat in an empty seat behind me. "Hello," he said to me.

"Hey," I said. "I'll ask you, then. What time is it?"

Napoleon looked deeply puzzled. He peered up at the very big and obvious white moon-face clock hanging at the front of the room.

"Aw," I said, "if you have to look at the clock, you're lost."

"I do not understand . . ." Napoleon started.

But Manny couldn't take it anymore. "It's freakin' Freddie time!" he blurted from inside his messy desk.

"Yesssss!" I said.

Freddie time.

Gold Dust time.

We had been waiting for this for a long time. Since 1918, to be exact. The arrival of Fred Lynn and Jim Rice to the Red Sox major league club. Everyone who knew the game knew that Lynn was going to be the best, ever. And that Rice was probably going to be the second best. The papers had already been calling them the Gold Dust Twins, the best pair of rookies ever to come along to one team in the same year. I had been charting their progress through the minor leagues since the Sox signed them, and finally, this was their year. And today. Today was the glorious first day, the ritual, where the huge eighteen-wheeler equipment trucks were packed up and dispatched to Winter Haven, Florida. Spring training. Every newscast in town showed footage of the trucks heading off. It was breathtaking.

Fred Lynn. My man. Breathtaking.

Jim Rice. Breathtaking.

Finally. Hallelujah.

"Excuse me?" Napoleon asked.

I ran through the whole scenario again. Happily. I half-hoped he would ask me to do it again.

"Oh," he said instead. "Baseball. I'm sorry, I don't follow baseball. I play cricket."

My turn. "Excuse me?"

He shrugged.

I had never even heard of this condition before.

"Everybody likes *baseball*," I pointed out.

"No, actually," he said politely but firmly. "Everybody does not."

Both Manny and Glen started laughing at this. Not loud mocking laughter, but the low, teasing, challenging kind. "So," Manny said in his exaggerated accent, "Meester Beisbol, whatchu gonna do about thees?"

I looked at Napoleon behind me, then over to Manny, then back to Napoleon. "I'm going to help him," I said calmly. "He needs help."

"I need no help, thank you."

"You'll be happier. . . ."

He scowled at me. "I am quite happy."

"Look," I said. Napoleon was turning out to be a kind of challenge, like a sneaky tough pitcher who kept making me hit fouls, and I had to figure him out. "These guys here were new once. They listened to me, and look at them now."

Glen gave a little embarrassed wave, and Manny a big, smiley one. It would be hard to notice now, but they really were raw material when the two of them moved in over on Fortuna Avenue five years ago. They didn't need a whole lot of work since they came from Cuba, where Louis Tiant came from, so baseball was already wired into them. But that didn't mean they hadn't come a long way, although I might have stretched it to say they did it by listening to me. Stretched it only a little, though.

As long as you have baseball on your side, you can overcome anything.

I just sort of hung there, turned around in my seat, smiling very friendly at Napoleon, like I was some kind of ambassador or something. He did not smile back. He did not do anything that I could tell. He was thinking.

"So then, the goal is to be like you? That is the key to happiness?"

I hadn't thought of it exactly that way before. Not in those very words. But hearing them now . . . I didn't know. A guy could do a lot worse.

I apparently had dwelled on this for a while without answering. "Turn around please," Napoleon said coolly.

"Call me when you need me," I said.

My concentration had been broken for too long now anyway. This was not like me, in late winter, sitting at my desk in school, before the start of lessons. I had to focus.

Fred Lynn. . . .

Fred Lynn. . . .

Fred Lynn. . . .

SNAP
CRACKLE
POP

The temptation is to say that it's a sound like nothing else in the world. But that wouldn't be true. There are variations on the sound that I make when I hit a ball with my bat just right, and all those variations have relatives out there in the non-baseball world.

There is the crack. It sounds so much like the sound a tree trunk makes when an old maple goes down that you have to take cover just in case. Jim Rice is already getting famous for the crack. They say that even coaches who have been in the game for forty years flinch when Rice cracks the ball like he does. When I hit a ball and it goes *crack*, that is as good as I can hit it. It might not be a home run because maybe I didn't get under it enough and it's a line drive, or maybe I got under it too much and it's a sky-high fly ball, but whether the thing gets out or not I am one happy and satisfied ballplayer because here is a secret I can share: I don't care a ton about scoring runs or winning games. What I care about is hitting a baseball.

Baseball is not about teamwork, no matter what anybody says. It is about pitching and catching and hitting a ball. Especially about hitting a ball. And all of those things get done by one guy alone. Baseball is a selfish game. I don't mind that. That's why it works.

There is the snap. If I am going with the pitch, like when Quin or Butchie is particularly cute with the curves and screwballs and I have to go with whatever I get, then bat-meets-ball is more like a snapping sound, a slapping sound, and I knock the thing into right field with less authority than I might like, but all the same it is very satisfying. Because that stuff can be devilishly hard to hit, and you have to be both smart and quick with your hands to change your stroke on the fly and get the ball out there in play. Fred Lynn does this, and I have seen it in the news. Balls you are sure he can't hit until, *smack*, there he goes, reaching out after it, putting the ball out there in play, and looking like he's just going to go with the flow and follow the thing right out there into the outfield, just to watch it land where he tells it to. The ball in play. I love the ball in play. I hate the ball in the catcher's hands.

Pop. Pop is a bad sound, the way I hear it. Because I hear it *pop*-pop. Double pop, like a mock. Because that to me is the sound of striking out, and striking out is the worst thing that can happen to a person. Anybody can miss a ball—*pop*—one time, because, sure, there are some good guys out there who can throw, and they can get lucky now and then. And if conditions are right for them and wrong for you, you can even get caught a second time—*pop*—and find yourself in jeopardy.

But a third strike. I have never been able to see the reasoning behind a third strike. Not in one at-bat, uh-uh, no way, no excuse. Nobody should be able to fool you or overwhelm you three times in one at-bat. No one. So the ultimate insult, the unbearable nightmare of a noise is the *pop*-pop of that third strike. The first *pop* being the ball landing in the catcher's mitt. The second being me banging the bat off my helmet.

Because striking out is not okay. Striking out means somebody else has the control. When the ball is over the plate, you should be able to hit it.

Nothing else makes sense.

The crack of the bat is churchbells to me. The sound of all is well.

SEVENTEEN
SQUARED

The arrival of the Ward 17s this past year was the first big import of new faces since Manny and all those guys came up from Cuba a few years back. But this bunch made even more of a difference, because the 17s didn't just bring new faces from outside the neighborhood, they brought *stuff*. Attitude. Butchie was a Ward 17 guy, and he was a good example of *stuff*. I could see where he might be a hard guy to handle, except for the baseball thing that got us together right away. He's a good ol' ballplayer. Mean pitcher. Loaded with intimidating, tough stuff.

But the everyday stuff mostly had to do with the fact that they weren't crazy about being here. All right, so it was school, so nobody was crazy about being here. But the 17s were the only ones who were here strictly because they didn't want to be someplace else. They were kind of angry about the busing deal and they didn't care who knew about it.

I didn't want to know about it.

"I can't stand this one more day," Butchie said, throwing his big self down into the desk next to me. He looked miserable, his long hair hanging straggly three inches below his ski hat. The hair, frozen as it was, looked like brown icicles.

"Hey Butch," I said casually, since it wasn't unlike him to be just like this. I knew his story. Everyone knew his story. He liked to tell his story anyway.

"Walk a half-mile. Take the bus to Forest Hills. Wait in the freezing cold for another stinking bus. Walk another two blocks. And for *what*?"

"To get to school?" I suggested.

Just then, Napoleon Charlie Ellis entered the room, walked the aisle, and took the seat on my right. Butch gestured through me, toward Napoleon.

"And why am I even doing this? Why am I even here? I'm sittin' with *them* anyway now, and tomorrow I'll probably be sittin' with more of 'em. Until my old man finds me a school *three* buses away."

Napoleon leaned forward, looked past me at Butchie, expressionless, but not without a message anyway. Butchie looked back.

"Forget about it," Butch said. "Nothing personal."

Napoleon shook his head. "Nothing personal? Tell me, is it that you think I am deaf, or that I'm stupid and cannot understand the words?"

I was now a hot sandwich.

"Of course it is personal," Napoleon went on. "You are talking about persons, and I am one of them. You traveled two buses to get here. So? I traveled two thousand miles. And to sit with *you*?"

"So who asked you to?" Butchie said. "It's not like we had a shortage of you people."

I did not want to be in the middle of this, but that is literally where I was. This did not have to happen. I had to do something.

"Listen," I said, making a slicing motion between them with my hand. "Butchie said forget about it. Didn't you hear that? He said forget about it. When a guy says forget about it, it's supposed to be the end of it, so . . . that's the end of it."

Butch was in deeper than he wanted to be anyway, I could see from his embarrassed red face. Of course I could see nothing of the kind on Napoleon's face. Napoleon had a different kind of face. I didn't really know Napoleon's face in that way.

But I assumed that he wouldn't want to be in this messiness. I assumed we would feel the same way. Wouldn't we?

Butch just turned away and sat rigid in his seat. I looked to Napoleon, who was slowly turning away as well.

"See," I said, "you just need to not make such a big deal out of stuff. Relax, Napoleon." I was hit with a timely inspiration from TV. "Like the commercial says, right? 'No problems.' Right? 'No prob-lems.'"

I thought I'd done pretty well, coming up with a smooth culture reference to ease things up. Maybe I knew more stuff than I gave myself credit for.

"That's the Bahamas," Napoleon said.

Now he didn't look too thrilled with me either. Cripes. It was all so unnecessary. I couldn't imagine it all wouldn't blow over by lunch.

Pre-lunch, down in the basement getting our food out of our lockers. There was a daily ritual, always brought the guys together no matter what kind of lousy day it was. Beating up on Arthur Brown's brown-bag lunch.

"Throw it here," I called to Butchie. Butchie lobbed me a perfect spiral, the length of the corridor and right through Arthur's outstretched hands. It was no fun unless Arthur at least had a shot at reaching it.

"Arthur, what's in here?" I asked, looking at the bag. "It's leaking already after only three passes."

"Tuna. Jerk," Arthur snapped, lunging my way.

Butchie was about to catch it, then let it fall. He loves that move. "Too much mayonnaise. We told you last time on tuna day, you gotta tell your mom to go easier on the mayo. Makes our hands all slippery. And it's making you too fat and slow to catch us."

"Give me my lunch," Arthur Brown growled at Butchie. He was very serious about it, which meant we only had three or four tosses left in the game. Butchie let it fly in my direction.

Just as I was about to catch it, a hand stuck up in my face, snagging the bag.

"Good grab, Napoleon," I said. Arthur was grimly

heading our way. "Here he comes," I said. "Unload, unload."

Butchie was waving his hands madly from the imaginary end zone. Arthur was bearing down on Napoleon.

Napoleon handed the bag to Arthur, who was so taken by surprise that he dropped it.

"What did you do that for?" I asked.

"It's the man's lunch," Napoleon said. "Is it not?"

Butchie was headed our way, quite disgusted at the turn of events. "What happened?"

"He gave me my lunch," Arthur said.

"Dope, whatja do that for?"

"Don't call me that," Napoleon said.

"You had no business doing that," Butchie said.

"Nevermind," I said. "He didn't know."

"What?" Napoleon Charlie Ellis wanted to know. "What did I not know?"

"What you did not know was that we have been doing this for a long time, and you weren't supposed to give Arthur back his lunch yet." Butchie was taking this very seriously, like we were some military outfit and the new scrub hadn't been read the rules. "For your information, Arthur *likes* this game and as a matter of fact he has been playing it for so long that he can't even eat right if he hasn't chased after his lunch for at least five minutes to stimulate his appetite. *Isn't that right*, Arthur?" Butch shouted, though straining in Napoleon's direction.

Everyone looked at Arthur.

"Um. I probably could eat it anyway."

Napoleon Charlie Ellis nodded, then walked to his own locker.

Butchie followed him. "So, you don't have to save him, *Charlie*, and you don't have to mess around with things you don't understand, like how things run here. Maybe you were in charge back in the school where nobody wore any shoes, but it ain't gonna be that way here."

Napoleon slammed his locker. That tin old-locker noise filled the concrete corridor and seemed to echo a hundred times.

"I did not ask you to call me Charlie. If you wish to talk to me you may do so, and you may call me Napoleon, and you may do it more quietly. I'll not be shouted at by *you*. And as for being boss of you, I have no ambition to be a pig farmer."

I had never seen anyone speak to Butch like this. I don't suppose Butch had ever seen it either, since the idea of it was making him go spastic.

"Who do you think you *are*, man. . . ." Butchie said, inching up too close and staring down at Napoleon from his extra few inches of height.

"I know well who I am," said Napoleon calmly, so calmly he nearly closed his eyes all the way as he said it.

This, I thought, was a good time to join in. I slipped between them.

"He just never played throw the lunch before, Butch," I said, giving him a healthy shove, but not so hard that he'd shove me back. Almost no one is allowed to shove Butchie. I am. But I'm not keenly interested in testing it beyond that. "He's still getting used to everything."

Butchie stared as I threw my arm around Napoleon's shoulders. Then Napoleon stared, at my arm. I don't think he was all that accustomed to this kind of contact. But he didn't do anything about it.

"Right," Butchie grunted. "Well, he better get used to everything. Quick." He turned to go back upstairs. He signaled Arthur Brown to follow, even though Butchie would not ordinarily be walking with Arthur. It was just one of those moments you're not supposed to walk away from alone.

"That boy has got a problem, Richard," Napoleon Charlie Ellis said.

"Butchie's just kind of . . . tense."

"He's not tense with you. He is tense with me."

"And *you*'re tense with *everybody*. Maybe the two of you are too much alike, what do you think of that?"

He removed my arm from his shoulders like he was removing a putrefied fish.

"You couldn't really believe that," he said, opening his locker again to get out his lunch.

"Well, you are kind of a hard guy yourself, Napoleon. It could just be that you make people be worse than they are, because of the way you are. Maybe it's you."

He closed the locker, stood with his own perfectly creased brown bag. It smelled incredible to me, all mixed and spiced, like Chinese food, only I couldn't imagine anybody bringing Chinese food for lunch, and anyway, it was a whole different spice smell.

"I am certain you do not believe such nonsense, Richard."

We headed over to my locker.

"Can we trade?" I asked. "Half of your lunch for half of mine? I never smelled a lunch like that in my life. I don't even want to know what it is. Can we trade?"

He sighed. "Possibly."

I opened my locker. It smelled like it usually does. Like Spam.

"No," he said immediately.

But as we walked up the stairs, he reached into his bag and handed me a small, breaded, spiced knot of some meat thing. I was almost afraid to eat it because that meant I wouldn't be able to smell it anymore.

"A gift," Napoleon Charlie Ellis said. "Now, please tell me you don't honestly believe . . ."

"Where was I?" I interrupted. "Oh yes, Jim Rice is going to be in left field, with Fred Lynn in center. They are talking about putting them number three and four in the lineup, with Rice batting cleanup. . . ."

"I am asking you to talk about something serious, Richard."

"Baseball is as serious as it gets," I said.

Napoleon shook his head, took a polite bite out of his food.

"Well it's as serious as *I* get anyway," I said, also taking a bite of his food.

STING

"So you've never played baseball," I said to Napoleon Charlie Ellis as we stood on a smooth slick coating of snow.

"I play cricket. As I said. Will I teach you?"

"Will you t—?" I practically choked on the thought. Somebody in North America teaching *me* what to do with a bat and ball. "Ah, ho-ho. Napoleon Charlie Ellis, we're gonna have big fun now."

"Now? No, not now. It is winter. In the spring and summer, then we will—"

I stood there shaking my head at him, and smiling. He shook his head in response, without smiling. I think I was making him a little nervous. "I don't believe in seasons," I said.

Napoleon Charlie Ellis looked past me, over my beloved and lovely field, still beloved and lovely with the snow continuing to come down over it. No matter. I knew what was under there, and it was beautiful.

"I don't know, Richard Riley Moncreif. If I lived here, I think I would believe in seasons."

I reached out and clapped him hard on the shoulder. It was a firm, square shoulder. "Excuse me? You *do* live here."

The shoulder sagged slightly, involuntarily. His face showed that his mind was off someplace else. A sudden small shock of sadness ran through me, like I had absorbed it by contact with Napoleon.

"Pretty warm in Dominica right now, I imagine."

He nodded.

"Stick with me," I said. "I know what you need. This situation," I waved my arm in a wide, sweeping circle over my hard-bit kingdom, where icicles climbed the chain-link backstop, and the pitcher's mound was no greater than any other petrified mound out there, "this situation is all about mind over reality. That's the trick. Remember, if you put your mind to it, you can do better than reality."

By now we were both staring off into white space.

"I am ready to put my mind to that," he said.

Sometimes, when it is cold, you have to connect perfectly to avoid the worst feeling in all the world. The buzzing electrified stinging of the hands after hitting the ball one eighth of an inch too high or low of the sweet spot. It would hurt less if, when you saw the pitch coming, you simply dropped the bat and smacked the ball with your bare hand. And if you really mess up and catch it either high up on the handle or way out on the very tip of the bat because one of the slickmasters like Butchie or Quin can't resist throwing the funny stuff in February, well, it's almost enough to put a guy off baseball for good.

Right, I know. Right about here is where I lose most people. I get the look, and the whole, aren't-you-taking-this-thing-a-little-too-seriously jag.

No. I am not. What really matters? It could be a million different things, and I don't necessarily have to appreciate what matters to somebody, except that I can appreciate that something does. Right, so, when I am hitting after a baseball, all I can tell you is that is what matters to me, and when I start my swing everything else there is falls away. School, family, friends and food and sky and grass are all gone to nowhere because I exist and the ball exists and that's pure.

Imagine the thing that matters. Imagine disappearing entirely into your thing that matters, needing *that* feeling. And then, *zinnngggg*.

It bites you. It hurts you so bad that you have to throw the bat on the ground, the same bat that has to be pried out of your hands some July days. That is not fair. Your own dog shouldn't maul you, and your bat shouldn't sting you. That's the world not right, right there.

I guessed Napoleon Charlie Ellis would like to avoid that feeling. He would need to be sheltered from the elements to start off.

"A batting *what*?" Napoleon said as we left the city proper on the bus north.

"Cage. It's a practice facility. Somebody invented this thing so that you could practice baseball against live pitching—well, sort of live—all day, all night, all year even if you were totally friendless and everything. Total baseball. Brings tears to my eyes just thinking about it."

"I will not be getting in any cage."

I had still not figured out Napoleon's style. He sounded so proper and serious whether he was doing Hail Marys at church or telling you about the rice and beans and fish he fed his dog.

"No, no, man it's not that kind of—"

"My uncle back in Dominica told me this would happen. He said if we dared come to this place, some white man would try to put me in a cage. . . ."

"That is *so* unfair . . . that hardly ever—"

The way he laughed, even, was so controlled you had to pay real close attention to catch him doing it to you. Napoleon Charlie Ellis was very good at being controlled. I would have to get better at paying attention.

"Fine," I said. "Wait 'til you get conked on the head with a pitch, then it's gonna be my turn to laugh."

"No it won't, because I will not be getting in any cage, Richard."

I knew there would be this initial slow period, an introductory phase. This was new to him, after all, this was foreign. But it was *baseball*. Even though Napoleon wasn't a regular player, I knew he had to be familiar with the game. And once familiar, well, like I said, this was *baseball*.

"You gotta love it," I said.

"No, actually. I don't *got ta*."

It was possible I was being mocked. But I'd have to let that slide because there were bigger issues at hand.

"Can you just trust me, Napoleon? Please? If you just give it a chance I am certain you are going to agree that baseball is *it*."

He paused, politely. Then spoke. "Cricket."

He couldn't have been serious, or if he was it was simply out of misinformation or improper training or some other form of messing up somebody did to the guy when he was supposed to be taught the critical fundamentals of life like crossing at the lights, four basic food groups, and baseball.

I paused long enough to let him gather his thoughts more properly. "Cricket," he repeated.

Right. What was I doing? Let him eat cricket.

"Okay," I said slowly, "look at it this way. You could spend your time playing one-man cricket, which I don't know the game but I figure is not a lot of fun, or you could take a shot at a game that you can play with lots of the guys."

Napoleon looked at me very seriously. He appeared to be choosing his words carefully, but when they came out they didn't sound all that carefully chosen. "From what I can see, Richard, I can't imagine why I would want to play with *the guys*." The way he snorted those words, *the guys*, it sounded as if he had a rocket of blue cheese crammed up his nose.

"You see there," I said, pointing at a spot on his chest, as if I was identifying *there*. "There you go. There you go being impossible. You could try, you know. You could just . . . try."

"Try," he echoed.

"Try."

"Why?"

Why. There's one for you. Why indeed? What was I doing? So what if I knew baseball was the key to life? That didn't mean he had to know it. So what if Napoleon Charlie Ellis seemed to be orbiting me for whatever reason since he showed up? That didn't make him my responsibility. As long as I had a field of live bodies around me in a game of baseball I never cared much whose bodies they were. So what difference did it make now?

My world was a pretty tight diamond-shaped thing before, first-second-third-home, and that worked fine for me. So if Napoleon didn't want to try, then fine. If he didn't want to get along, then fine. That was his right. He didn't want to change his way and I didn't want to change mine. Fine. We really didn't need to do this. We didn't need anything.

"You gonna play ball with me, or what?" I snapped.

"Yes I am," he snapped.

When we had paid our money and taken up residence in the cage, I decided the best thing I could do for my man to start him out was to lead by example. I handed Napoleon the bucket of balls and nodded toward the pitching machine.

"See what I'm doing here with my feet, Napoleon?" I asked. He was staring at me, but not at my feet.

"How did we decide that you would go first?"

"What? Of course I'm going first. I'm leading by example."

"I know how to swing a bat."

"Ya, but I'm going to show you the right way."

I could see his one eyebrow go way up higher than the other and disappear under his shiny red batter's helmet. "You mean you are going to show me *your* way."

"Right," I said. "The right way." This time I didn't look at him long enough to give him a chance to be difficult. If we were going to do this right, I was going to have to let a lot of Napoleon's stuff just pass me by. Later, when he was great, he'd thank me for it. I looked down and began scratching in the dirt with my feet like a bull about to charge.

"Why do you do that thing with your feet like a chicken?"

I stood back out of the box. "Like a bull, Napoleon. I do it like a bull, not like a chicken. And I do it to get a good firm grip of the earth beneath me."

"I see. Without it you will slip off the earth, is that it?"

Clearly it was time to block out the taunting and concentrate on the important business of addressing the ball. One of the many critical skills you learn from baseball is to focus on the job no matter what kind of nonsense people are talking at you.

There is no room in the game for the junk parts of life. That's why the game is better than life.

My feet planted like oak roots, my helmet screwed down tight, my hands gripping the handle of my thirty-ounce bat tight enough to control it, loose enough to maintain the right *feel*. The heel of my left hand was flush up against the butt of the bat handle. I don't like to choke up. You are lost in the universe if you're choking up, and if you don't know where you are in the universe how can you ever expect to hit a well-thrown ball? If you feel like you need to choke up you should just move to a smaller bat. Bat's too heavy, then you're too cocky. You embarrass yourself. Bat's too light, you got no confidence. You embarrass yourself. And if there is no bat small enough for you then you aren't ready to play so sit down for another year or two.

I have always taken the time to select the bat I could really hit with.

I was by now staring hard at the machine just the same as if it were a real flesh-and-bone pitcher. Searching for its eyes. It was humming, ready. I could not wait. From my hair to my fingertips to my clenching solar plexus to my twitching thighs, I was ready for this, like the first pitch of the World Series.

Like *every* pitch.

"Okay," I called, "start feeding balls into that slot in back." Napoleon did, and started it all coming.

Sling, it came. Hopping, spinning, straight. I felt what was almost a laugh come up out of me as I went after it, because I was so excited, and because the pitch was so fat and easy.

Whiff. I missed it by half a foot, and nearly screwed myself into the ground to boot. The place was like a combination airplane hangar/gym, and all the noises were exaggerated a thousand echoey times since we were the only people there. Like the sound of a swing and a miss, whiffing loudly around the place.

And the sound of the razz.

"That is the right way then? I think I can do that, Richard. I could do that when I was very little. I guess I am what you would call a natural, then."

I hadn't yet taught him the razz, so maybe he *was* a natural. All the more reason to ignore him.

I dug and dug my feet in again, into the batter's box dirt, the only bit of natural ball field in the place. But just the right bit, the part the hitter makes contact with, feels his way into, connects himself to. With my feet in the dirt I always had the old feeling, that I was where I needed to be, whether I was playing under the lights at night in August, in the sun in June, on the crusted ground of

February, or even this indoor weirdness. Feet in the dirt, hands wrapped just so around the bat handle. The rest was just a matter of time.

Humm, sling, on it came, and this time there was no laugh, no urge, no childish lapse of concentration. There was instead the crack. I never felt a thing, as the ball gave itself up to the very meatiest sweet spot way out on the bat barrel, and I did what a hitter is supposed to do. I hit.

The ball hissed as it sailed into the netting about twenty yards from the plate. It felt so good, my attention slipped once more as I stupidly paused to dwell on what had already disappeared into the net, and into the past.

Humm, sling, the next ball was on its way, my way, and I was just getting the bat up off my shoulder by the time the ball went past. Out of instinct, I made a lame wave at the pitch anyway, looking totally foolish and accomplishing less than nothing. It would have been wise to just let it pass, but that kind of wisdom has always come hard to me. I have trouble letting a pitch go by unmolested. Even a bad pitch.

"You tell me you have played this game before, is that right?"

Napoleon Charlie Ellis's rag-the-batter skills were suspiciously well developed. I was going to have to watch him for other surprises.

He was good for me, though. Because that was the last of my breakdowns. For the next ten minutes solid, not a thing got past me. I hit a few squibs, a few fouls, a grounder and a fly ball, but I did not once swing without making contact with that ball. And not a one of those swings was halfway. I had my stroke in place, dropping my right shoulder at just the point of contact, torquing slightly in reverse before uncorking, with the bat on a straight plane the whole way, level to the ground and the roof of the sky. Or in this case, the roof of the roof.

It is really a simple thing, if you pay attention. I often wonder why everyone cannot figure out something so beautifully simple as hitting.

The more I swung, the more controlled and stronger I got. And the quieter Napoleon Charlie Ellis got. I could feel him there behind the machine, and after five years in the Regan Youth League, I had come to know the difference between the various kinds of noise and silence. Some guys will shut up when you've got it going just because they begrudge it, and won't give you the satisfaction. But some are better than that.

"That . . . was remarkable," Napoleon said. "You are so aggressive, the way you do that, like you have something personal against the ball."

"I don't," I said, trying not to smile too much though his words felt pretty all right. "I love the ball. I just want to knock the skin off it."

"And now it is my turn."

"Yessirree," I said, and handed him my bat.

He took it, looked at it. Ran his hand up and down the

smoothness of it, and checked the inscriptions. Most kids went with Louisville Slugger, but I preferred Adirondack. He balanced it in one hand, then worked the grip. It was obvious that there was a foreignness about the bat to Napoleon, but it was also obvious that he appreciated a fine instrument. You could tell, in the way he was *thinking* about the feeling of the bat, measuring, stroking, examining it, rather than just grabbing it. He was treating the Adirondack right.

I liked that. Felt something like grateful about it.

"The bat is so different," he said, smiling in a kind of wonderment. "The cricket bat is flat."

"Fl—" I shook my head, in a definite wonderment. "How are you supposed to get a good whack at anything with a flat bat? Jeez. I mean it, Napoleon, I think I got to you just in time."

I was still messing, but it was nearly the point where we had to cross over into serious business. The flat bat and all the other weirdnesses that followed my friend north were interesting, but I really thought I could help him recover from it all just the same.

"Will I show you?" I said carefully. I was careful because, while I might think I know everything in the world about hitting, I also know a guy can be pretty touchy about being shown stuff, when it comes down to it. Particularly when that guy tends to be touchy about just about everything.

"Why don't I try it myself first."

Like that. He's stubborn, okay. I would have said the same thing myself.

First he tried doing what I did in the batter's box, scuffing and digging first with one shoe, then the other. He didn't get very far before breaking down in hysterics. "It's just too silly," he said, shrugging and letting the bat fall to his side.

I marched right over. "That's because you are doing a Carlton Fisk," I said, and went into Fisk's famously weird and endless preparations of twisting one foot just so, like he was planting a rare delicate tulip bulb, then, about five minutes later, plant the second one. Then he did this sort of wiggle dance with his enormous behind—he wasn't a fat guy, actually, just a guy with an uncommonly broad backside—then he would look at his bat, as if they had never met before, wave it a couple of times to see if it was loaded. Then he would address the pitcher.

"You don't need to do a Fisk. Do a Yaz instead." And I showed Napoleon what Captain Carl Yastrzemski did, which was basically stand like a tree with his bat raised as high above his head as he could manage while still facing the pitcher. It was hugely impractical, but it was a kind of monumental thing, like a statue to the art of hitting, and something every kid in Boston tried at least once.

"What about these twins people you keep talking about, Rice and Lynn. Maybe I should do them."

"Can't," I said crisply.

"Why not?"

"Because I am Lynn," I said.

"Ah. I see. Mr. Rice then?"

I thought about that. It was true that Jim Rice had an ungodly beautiful stroke. It was as if he didn't even use his arms—great big arms, I might add—but just flicked his wrists. And still, his ball went a mile. This would of course be a great thing to copy. But it was all but impossible, especially for a beginner.

"Can't be done," I said with complete authority.

"I see," he said, nodding. "You mean *you* can't do it."

"*I* can't . . . *I* . . . ?"

"That's all right," Napoleon assured me. "I will watch him on television and teach myself. For now I will improvise."

I huffed, "I can't . . . huh. . . ." and went out to the machine.

And he did improvise. Looked almost natural, but a little stiff at the same time, as Napoleon crouched just slightly, leaning over the plate. His hand position was good, the two mitts pressed together and held midchest high. He had a hard concentration look on as he let out a short quick bark to get me to feed the first ball.

He looked so tough. I wanted to throw the ball myself. That's what always happened when I saw an honest-to-god hitter. I wanted to go after him, to try and beat him, to pay my respect. Right now it made me just want to shove the machine aside and try to strike Napoleon out on my own.

He looked ready.

He looked like he meant business.

I fed the beast and the first pitch came winging his way.

He looked *lost*.

The first swing—if you could call it that—I saw Napoleon Charlie Ellis take was like an apology in motion. It looked more like he was trying to use that fine piece of ash to kill a beetle at his feet, and I could tell he was embarrassed. But he curled himself right back into his stance. It was early season, even for me, and Napoleon was totally new. He'd get better.

But not in the immediate future, I thought. The only reason his second cut was not worse than his first was that it was impossible to get worse than that first one. Not that he didn't make the effort. His bat speed improved, but probably more out of anger than confidence. He missed the ball by so much, he may have had his eyes closed. A lot of little kids will do that when they swing their hardest, close their eyes midway through from the effort. I hoped Napoleon Charlie Ellis was not an eye-closer at this late age.

"I could crank the speed down a little," I said.

I was only trying to help.

Napoleon turned, hands on his hips, and glared at me so hard I thought he was going to come after me with the bat. He held the look long enough for the machine to send two more pitches sailing into the fence. I was still doing my job anyway. Not that it would have made any difference if Napoleon was there to wave at it.

"I do not need it slow," Napoleon snapped. "I am just having a bit of difficulty seeing the ball as it leaves the machine."

"A bit?" I said. "I don't think you could miss worse if the machine was throwing M&M's."

Which was not helpful, probably. He glared at me a little harder, then drew his glasses out of their case, out of his shirt pocket.

Back in the box. Digging with one foot, digging with the other. Upright, hands high. Staring down the machine.

Whiff. He missed cleanly. But this was not like before. This looked like he had swung a bat before.

"So this really is your first time. You never played baseball, even once?" I asked.

"Never. Cricket," he said. "This bat feels strange to me."

The ball came over the plate. He swung late and fouled one off.

"Well, it's the way a bat should feel," I said.

"It is very light," he said.

Excuse me? *My* bat, light?

He was starting to develop something of a rhythm now, and while he was still mostly missing or fouling pitches, he was at least ready to hit when the ball arrived. And his swing was strong and fluid. Napoleon was an athlete of some kind, that I could tell. Even if he was wasting his body on something as weird as cricket. He could probably learn the game if he wanted to. His swing was nice to watch.

Know what else was nice to watch? His foul balls and dribblers and weak pop-ups. I always loved to see a new player around here, because I love to play so much, and there are never enough players to get up a game on a given day in late August, October, March.

But I also love none of those players being better than me. I cannot help that. I cannot help it. I want to be the best, with loads of other players right behind me. But behind me.

Yet I wanted him to get better. I wanted him to get it. I was looking at Napoleon, and I was seeing a guy who should be a ballplayer. A fine ballplayer.

Napoleon Charlie Ellis's swing was straightening out into something pretty, and powerful. But he had a funny little balance problem which I was sure came from the oddities of cricket, and which would prevent him from ever hitting a baseball as well as he could.

I fed the machine and watched him grit his teeth. I fed the machine and watched him adjust his eyeglasses. I fed the machine and watched him grip the bat handle harder and throw himself at the ball, and I fed the machine and watched him foul off one pitch after another only to straighten up and get ready to do it again and again.

I began watching his face more than his hands or his balance, and I began to see something familiar. I began to see Napoleon's approach to the ball, his *need* to hit the ball at the moment it was there to be hit.

I stopped feeding the machine. I walked around it and walked to Napoleon Charlie Ellis, who stood frozen, eyeing me suspiciously.

I got right up behind him, right at his back, and reached around him with both arms so that we were both gripping the bat. Then I leaned us both back away from the pitcher's mound, taking some weight off our front feet, changing our balance completely.

"Nothing personal," I said.

"No. Nothing personal."

"Feel that?" I said. "Feel the difference there?"

He didn't say anything, but I could feel in the way he bounced lightly on the rear leg.

He got it. He shifted, back, forth, back, forth, feeling the difference. He swung, replanted, swung. He held his stance and stared ahead, visualizing the pitch, then swinging through the invisible ball.

Finally, he allowed himself a small grin.

"See," I said. "See what cricket almost did to you? Good thing I showed up."

"Go on, feed the machine," he said, already crouching, coiled, waiting to let loose.

GIRL

17

As a rule, I don't like exceptions. I like rules.

Beverly, however, was an exception. We called her "Redheaded Beverly" to distinguish her from regular Beverly. Regular Beverly had sandy hair and had attended St. C's since first grade and walked to school because she was from the neighborhood. Redheaded Beverly, on the other hand, was interesting and weird and not like anybody else.

One of the ways she was different was that she was a Ward 17, the only girl 17, so the lifelong St. Colmcille's Community kids never completely seemed to *get* her. Another way she was different was that nobody from Ward 17 seemed to get her either.

We were talking, Redheaded Beverly and I, in the schoolyard, which we did most mornings before the bell. It was the best place and time to talk to a girl, because it was almost as if you weren't doing it. The entire population of St. C's students was out and buzzing, acting the

nutters, playing throwball or pitching pennies or just running around headless. And though you never could find
out who was doing it, it was a constant that there was mad
screaming going on at all times in the schoolyard.

So while you wouldn't think it was possible, you
could actually exist in this little bubble in the center of all
that and have real conversations with real people—even if
they were girls—in the middle of all that.

"I like baseball fine," she said, "but I don't think it is
the most important thing in the whole world, like you do."

I took a shot. "I don't think it's *the* most important
thing in the whole world, Beverly."

"Yes you do."

Should I try again? Could I?

"Well it *is*," I said.

Here's one of those things about Beverly that's pretty
decent. She wouldn't fight with you. If she disagreed and
wanted to let you know that but still get on with the conversation, she would say blah-blah-blah.

"Blah-blah-blah. But if it were me, and I were trying to
show a person new to the country what it was all about
here, I'd take him to the symphony. Boston has one of the
world's greatest orchestras. Their conductor, Seiji Ozawa,
is a huge international superstar."

"Um, *Ozawa*? Sorry Bev, but if I'm going to introduce
my friend to American culture, I'll probably start out with
people who at least *sound* like they're American."

"Oh, like Carl Yastrzemski."

"Exactly."

"Dur, Richard. Like there were more Yastrzemskis than Ozawas at the Battle of Bunker Hill, is that it?"

"Well," I said after careful thought, "probably. . . ."

"Blah-blah-blah. There were *exactly* the same number."

Sister Jacqueline, the principal and my homeroom teacher, appeared then in the yard with her mighty bell. That meant in a few minutes she'd be clanging away and we would have to line up.

"Okay Mr. All-American, I'll make you a deal. Let's take a quick poll, right here in the yard. I'll bet you a buck more kids can spell Ozawa than Yastrzemski."

I was about to let out a loud mock of a laugh but quickly, as my mouth hung open, made a stab at the spelling myself. Uh-oh.

"Carl Yastrzemski is an American institution," I said instead. "And I don't think you have any right—"

"You can't spell it either, huh?"

She was always like this. Difficult. Always making things complicated. Regular Beverly would have understood better.

"Read the papers," I said. "*Real* Americans call him Yaz."

"I'll go one step further, even," she pressed. "If you can find me more people who can spell Yastrzemski than can spell Ozawa, then I will go with you and Napoleon to a Red Sox game."

Now *this* was an offer. I was a little nervous—we

weren't talking about Carl *Smith* here after all—but more excited. And I had to have faith that my people could do this. I clapped.

"However," Beverly said, "if I win, you know where the three of us will be going, don't you?"

Rats.

Together we began the test. Beverly and I started patrolling the yard trying to collar kids for the quiz. But even that proved difficult because the very sight of Sister Jacqueline and her bell set the whole place into extra rev motion as everybody tried to squeeze the last drops of pre-boring school life out of life.

"Yo! Hey. Whoa. You there." We tried, but nobody had the time.

And I was increasingly pleased. Yastrzemski. Yastrzemski? What was I thinking? The girls I knew mostly had no interest in baseball, and the boys had enough on their plates trying to spell their *own* names. I was starting to picture myself sitting in Symphony Hall, in a coma.

Ring, bell, ring.

I have to admit, I lost my nerve so badly I finally angled our search over toward Sister Jacqueline, who had gotten herself wrapped up in a conversation with the custodian, Mr. Mendelson, and had drifted past bell-ringing time.

"Sister," I said. "Aren't we late?"

Sister took a quick gander at her watch, and sure enough started pumping that big brass beautiful bell so hard it was as if she thought she could pull back that lost ninety seconds of our education with the force of it.

"Chicken," Beverly said to me. Then she topped me. Went straight to the top.

"Okay then," Sister said. "That's a good one. Let's see. O-Z-A-W-A."

"Ya rat," I whispered to Beverly.

"And Y-A-S-T-R-Z-E-M-S-K-I."

Nuns. Is there anything they can't do? I sighed with relief. Tie. Bet's off. Until . . .

"O-Z-A-" Mr. Mendelson began, after Sister called him back from his appointed rounds.

One right.

"Y-E-Z—"

Come on, Mendelson, ya fink.

"This is fun, and an interesting point, Beverly," Sister Jacqueline said. "Let's take it inside and try it out on the whole class."

Very bad idea. "Wait, wait, no, Beverly, we forgot to add first names. They have to spell the first names too. For me, Carl. For you, Seiji."

The two of them ganged up on me and shot down my proposal. Shot down even more mercilessly was my chance in the bet. I got creamed. Of the thirty-two kids in our class, about one quarter got neither name right. Four got both right.

But in the important swing-vote category . . . I stopped counting the correct Ozawas once the figure reached twenty. As for Captain Carl . . . several boys punted and tried to get away with spelling Yaz. I figured after fifteen years in a Red Sox uniform it was high time he Americanized it anyway, but Sister did not agree. One girl began the spelling with a U. A couple more went straight from the Y to the S. Almost nobody could figure out what to do with the stupid Z, and to tell you the truth by the end I was angry enough at the guy to agree with them. He even threw us by *moving* the Z into a whole nother spot when he nicknamed himself, which I also mentioned in my defense, with no success.

Sister made great use of the opportunity, turning the contest into a fascinating progression of phonetic, geographic, and civic lessons. She led a discussion on what constitutes culture, and what constitutes "American." It was all very nice and all very interesting, and gave a person no extra citizenship points for being a baseball player. She was clearly biased.

Which was fine for Sister Jacqueline. She didn't have to go to the stupid symphony.

Napoleon Charlie Ellis was late that morning. He walked into the middle of the discussion and took his seat next to mine at the back of the class. Sister caught him on the fly, pulling him right in.

He got them both right.

MULLIGATAWNY
SOUP

"I never told you about my family, did I?"

I was almost at school, enjoying a fairly blissful crisp and lonely walk through crusted thin snow. I normally walked alone to school, which was fine with me, and there were some days that felt more alone than others. This had been one of them, and it was welcome. It wasn't cold in my head that morning, it was balmy. And it wasn't white or slushy brown, it was green, everywhere, ragweedy and dewy. To be honest, Boston during the months after Christmas and before Easter can be nobody's paradise, and it's good if you can imagine yourself someplace better. I can do that, have always been able to. I'm lucky, I figure.

But it helps to be alone.

"I said, I never told you about my family," Napoleon repeated. He was a bit winded, apparently from catching up to me. That cold air will cut up the lungs some days, especially if you're not used to it.

I heard him the first time, but I was not being rude. It

was more like when you're being woken up for school, you don't want to be, but you are being shaken and shouted at, and it takes some time before you can get the hearing thing and the responding thing together.

"I never asked," I said. "Figured it was your business."

"I don't mind discussing it."

"You don't have to, though. It's okay."

"I don't mind, actually."

Jeez. What did I do? One second, there I was camped under a nice simple fly ball with a warm breeze in my face, and the next second I'm wrapped up in a guy's family. I didn't want to be wrapped up in any guy's family.

"Sure, Napoleon, tell me about your family," I said, even if this all sounded weird and unnecessary to me. I knew all I needed to know about everybody. And everybody knew all they needed to know about me. That was the joy of never going anywhere, never meeting anyone. Unfortunately, I supposed, Napoleon had to be allowed a little catching up. But just a little.

"I am only here with my father," he said. "My mother stayed in Dominica with my older brother, Neville. He is going to graduate this term, and so they decided to stay until the end of the school year. My father had to start his job this term, so it was decided we would come now, together, and I would begin getting settled in school, meeting people. . . ."

I looked at him. I pointed at myself. "Me. You needed to get a jump on meeting me?"

"Yes," he said, fighting a little smile. He usually didn't

have to fight all that hard, as smiles didn't often attack Napoleon. Not since he'd been in Boston at least.

"So then, what, did you just wake up this morning with the urge to tell me about your family?"

"No," he said. Thought about it. "Yes," he said. Then, "No."

"Hey Napoleon, you want me to leave while you settle this amongst yourselves?"

"No," he said, closing his eyes, getting himself together. He didn't have long. We were almost at school.

"It's my father . . . he worries . . . that I might not be, meeting people. Might not be, acclimating, settling in. That I'm not getting along socially."

"I see," I said. "Um, well he's right, isn't he?"

"I *know* he is right," he snapped.

We were at the school doors. I got there first, held the door for Napoleon. I spoke as he walked past me. "And so instead of getting to know a lot of people a little bit, you're going to try and get to know one person a lot? I don't think it works like—"

"So then tell me about your family."

Oh, no. This was really not my idea of chat. *No batter, no batter. Humm, baby. I got it, I got it.* That's my idea of a personal statement.

"Relax, will you?" I said, stalling. "Your dad's not gonna quiz you tonight, is he?"

"I cannot relax. There is no time. Are you my friend?"

I did not think I had ever been asked that by anybody.

If pressed, I would have said that I didn't think anybody, anywhere had ever been asked that question. Not for real, anyhow. Not unless it was a joke. Why would anybody have to ask a question like that? You would just sort of know, wouldn't you? If a person feels like a friend, that's a friend, and you find yourself hanging out together, so you just do it and don't ask questions. And if a person doesn't feel like a friend then you would kind of know that too and you wouldn't be spending time with them and so the business of asking wouldn't be likely to come up anyhow. And if you weren't sure?

If you weren't sure, I would figure the question would be too embarrassing to ask.

Napoleon Charlie Ellis stared at me.

The bell started clanging away.

"We have to get inside," I said.

He continued with the staring thing. Staring me down with that expression that seemed to have loads of questions and demands in it. Working me with eyes that could peel layers off you like acid, until you gave up, answered him, confessed.

"Ya, I'm your friend. All right? Can we go inside?"

"Good," he said, brushing past all businesslike, like he didn't care all that much anyway. Which, I didn't know a lot, but I knew that was a lie. "Good," he repeated, "because I told my father you were."

I followed him in. So? was what I was thinking. Was this really that big a deal?

I didn't ask him out loud, though. I was afraid he would answer.

"We have a special surprise for you this morning," Sister Jacqueline said. "A speaker."

We don't all speak with one voice often in Sister Jacqueline's class, but she can always bring us together with the simple mention of the word "speaker." I think it's middle C we all groan in.

"I think we can do better than that," she said, unfazed by our lack of enthusiasm. "Our guest this morning is one of the world's leading authorities in his field. . . ."

"In his field? We gotta listen to a farmer speech?" Manuel asked.

Everybody laughed. Even Sister Jacqueline laughed. This was one of the better elements of being here in St. C's, at least in this particular class. Sister ran a fairly loose ship, and as long as we didn't take liberties, we were allowed some floor. Especially if you were funny, you were allowed some floor. Manny had the floor a lot.

"No, as a matter of fact, our guest's field is literature."

We reached high C with that groan.

"He is a professor of creative writing and Caribbean literature over at Boston University, and has generously donated his time to . . ."

Sister continued her glowing introduction, but my attention was pulled by Napoleon slinking down in his seat and covering his eyes.

"What's up with you?" I asked.

"My father," he said.

"Really? That's him? Cool."

"Yes? How would you like for your father to come and speak to your classmates?"

"And what, lecture us about mufflers and brake pads? I'd love to see him try. No, my man, you're the lucky one. This'll be fun." I reached over and gave Napoleon's forearm a squeeze.

"Please, let it not be fun," Napoleon said.

"Sorry, that's out of my control," I said.

". . . welcome Doctor Malcolm Ellis," Sister concluded, as Dr. Ellis strode into the room and we all politely clapped for him.

He was a serious-looking guy, about six foot one, with a lean face that had sharp angles like it was carved from stone, tightly cut graying hair, a trim mustache, and black frame glasses. He wore a pearly gray overcoat that he removed to reveal a dark blue suit with a vest. And a long scarf. Sister took his things and disappeared, leaving Dr. Ellis to us. We were silent, and more polite than we were for the average speaker, as he looked us over, expressionless. Then he smiled, and an entirely different face opened up as the flesh of his face rose and inflated, making roundness where there were those hard edges before.

Manny raised his hand. Dr. Ellis nodded at him.

"Doctor, I have this problem with nosebleeds—"

"Try cutting your fingernails shorter, son," he

answered before Manny could even close his mouth.

We love Manny. But we love to see Manny get topped. Most of the class laughed out loud, and clapped. But not everyone.

"I rode two buses to see a minstrel show," somebody from the back said in a low voice. Napoleon glanced over his shoulder, then faced front again.

"Good one, Doc," Manny said, pointing at the speaker. "I like that. Can I have it?"

"You may if you can tell me what it would be called if you appropriated my work in writing, without permission."

"Plagiarism," Manny shot back.

"Ah, we are a well prepared group. That is good. For I am really only here to check the quality of my son's education." The broad smile opened wider as Dr. Ellis peered down at his son. His son smiled weakly. Everyone looked at Napoleon now.

But, aside from the basic and obvious fact that it was the guy's father, there seemed to be no reason to be embarrassed. As far as speakers went, the good doctor was not bad.

He launched into a history of Caribbean literature, which didn't figure to be on any test so I didn't listen too hard. But what I did catch, and found impossible to ignore, was the sound of him. He spoke with a style, with a kind of music to him that was enough to hold some part of your attention no matter how boring his subject was.

He seemed to hum, as he spoke, and sometimes to be laughing although I would catch this and look up and find that he wasn't laughing at all but was in fact speaking intensely on some bit of literature that even the best of our students cared about only a little and the rest of us couldn't even fake. There were moments when you could have been pulled all the way in, when he talked about somebody named Lovelace, and some mad-sounding book with dragons and carnivals and when he was whipping it up you thought, Get me that book. Until you realized Dr. Ellis was performing, selling little bits of a thing like they did in commercials, and the thing itself was going to wind up meaning all but nothing to the likes of you, so reading an entire book of it was out of the question.

You wanted to believe him, you wanted to care, and you could, if you didn't worry too much about the message and just listened to the way he would swing through certain words, like "forward," which came out like *far-ward*, and "the minister of finance," which rolled out as *dee meencestah of fee-naanse*. It sounded very slick to me, and I noticed somehow his hands did a sort of mime version of the same thing as he sang the words accompanied by a fluttering of those hands—birdlike toward the ceiling, then a quick loud *clap*, then a challenging long finger in somebody's face, then all our faces as he spanned the room asking, "You think so? I think so. You think so?" to one obscure literary idea or another.

I had never heard anybody like Dr. Ellis before. Right, I was sitting next to his son, but just the same, I felt as if I had never heard it before, in any form. Why? I looked over to Napoleon. "He's great," I whispered.

Napoleon nodded. He smiled, and I could tell he was proud. But then the smile slipped away. If it was me I would have held it a little longer.

I went back to listening to sounds instead of ideas, and found myself so lulled by him that I was caught flat when he asked for questions. There was a bit of a silence, followed by the whispering, as people tried coming up with questions that had some thin connection to what the doctor had been talking about for the last half hour. I looked up at the small box of a window at the front door of the class to see framed in it the soft and kind but not-too-pleased face of Sister Jacqueline. It was considered terrible form not to ask our guest speakers a slew of informed questions, and if we didn't, the scene after he left would not be pretty.

Miraculous Manny rescued us for a start.

"The way you speak, it's almost a singsong, more like a little kid than an adult."

Dr. Ellis was pleased. "I am not an adult, I am a writer."

"Hah," Manny said. Manny was developing a new hero. Unfortunately he was not developing any follow-up questions.

"Ask him what forms he writes in," came the quiet, island-inflected voice on my right. Again, it made me think of the differences in their speech, father and son. Napoleon was so much more . . . controlled.

"I write realism," Dr. Ellis said, "until realism wearies me. Then I write fables, allegories, plays, songs, verse, essays, and letters to my friends. But in the end, I write about the same two things. The same two things, I think, that everyone writes about. I write about my dreams, and about my doubts. Dreams and doubts, they will keep a person's mind occupied for a great long while."

There was silence then. Sister was smiling, pleased, in her window, like a big canary in a small cage.

"And mulligatawny," he added.

More silence.

"Mulligatawny. It has a lovely sound, does it not? I have always loved the sound of mulligatawny, the very loveliness of the syllables, the play in there. And it is a very fine soup. As words, it is beautiful, mulligatawny, as food it is beautiful, mulligatawny, so it fills me twice. I write about mulligatawny whenever I can because *that* is what it is all about. I keep a can on my desk even, for inspiration."

After a brief pause, Dr. Ellis thanked us and we broke into applause. "Really, Napoleon," I could say louder now with the cover of hands clapping, "he's great."

Napoleon Charlie Ellis was smiling again, but still looking not too sure about it. "Yes, well, you would be less enthusiastic if you had to eat mulligatawny four times per week. I am missing my mother's cooking." He waited. But he wasn't finished. "I am missing my mother."

I was in no doubt about what was the right thing to do then.

I looked away.

We were allowed to buzz for a few minutes after we had a speaker, so Sister could chat with them, ask all the questions we hadn't, and basically butter them up enough to come back for another free visit next year. While this was going on, we suddenly got the call. Sister was motioning for Napoleon to come up, and when he did, to my surprise, he tugged a chunk of my shirt sleeve to haul me along.

"Hello, sir," I said. "Nice talk."

"Thank you, Mr. Moncreif," Dr. Ellis said, shaking my hand.

I stood there like a dummy.

"Napoleon has talked quite a bit about you. Says you are a fine baseball player."

Wa-hoo. Familiar territory. "Well, yes sir, I do love baseball. I play all the time. I want to get Napoleon playing too, as much as I can. Do you like baseball?"

He smiled at me, checked his watch. Sister Jacqueline rolled her eyes and bugged them at me at the same time, which is quite a sight. She was giving me the old ix-nay on the oring-bay aseball-bay face. Like I really bore all our speakers into never returning.

"Yes, as a matter of fact I have followed it somewhat. But I plan to watch a lot more of it this season since I am working so close to Fenway Park and all. Do you know I can see the Citgo sign from my office window?"

I gasped. I actually did. "Napoleon never told me that. You never told me that."

Napoleon sighed. "I was saving it." He sounded a little sarcastic.

"Anyway," Dr. Ellis said, though it sounded more like *ahh-na-wey*. "I must be going. But I thought it was time I met you. And we will continue our discussion at the dinner. I am looking forward to it."

I was completely lost. But I had never heard of a student at St. C's contradicting an adult on school property, in front of a nun, and living to tell the tale. Not even a normal adult, never mind a big-time international speaker with a "Doctor" at the front of his name.

"I'm looking forward to it too."

I looked at Napoleon out of the corner of my eye. He looked away with his entire face.

We were walking home together.

"You don't have to go," he said quietly. He sounded embarrassed.

"Why wouldn't I want to go?" I had never been to a restaurant in my life. Not a proper one anyway, that took reservations and credit cards and stuff. Never really wanted to go to one either.

He shrugged. "I don't know. Maybe the whole thing is . . . foolish."

"Nah," I said. "No it isn't. We'll go. It'll be fine. Where are we going to go?"

"Someplace called Anthony's Pier Four."

"Whoa," I said. "Pier. That means water. That means fish. Is this going to be a fish place? Am I going to have to eat fish?"

"What is wrong with fish? Fish is wonderful food."

"Fish is what people eat when they can't find any real food. It's like disaster food."

As he often, mysteriously does, Napoleon seemed to take this personally. "I am sure they will have some meat for you."

"Cool," I said.

We walked in silence for a bit.

"So, you picked me," I said, in a sort of wonder.

"My father wanted to get acquainted with my circle. You are my circle."

My first impulse was, I wanted to make a joke about that. I had to. I looked at Napoleon.

"Thanks," I said.

The whole day he had seemed off. Unsure of himself. Not as rigid or as hard as I had come to expect. I figured his father had done that by showing up. If my father had shown up, my day would have been thrown off too.

"Can I ask you a question, Napoleon?" I said. When he didn't say anything, I asked it anyway. "How come your accent's not as strong as your dad's?"

Napoleon looked me face-on, right into my eyes, and

he looked hard and grim, and suddenly old. His voice came out very flat.

"Worlds within worlds," he said.

I didn't even try. "Huh?"

"Because we function in our own worlds, even though we live in essentially the same place. My father is in the business of being West Indian, and people everywhere love him for it. While his son, on the other hand, spends his days in a place where it would be better not to make a point of it."

"What? What do you mean? What are you talking about?"

What came next was the first harsh thing Napoleon Charlie Ellis or Richard Riley Moncreif ever said to each other.

"How stupid are you, Richard, may I ask?"

My first response was—I could feel it even if I couldn't see it—to go all red in the face. My second was to walk faster and try to leave Napoleon behind.

"No, no, listen to me," he said, staying with me.

"No. I don't want to listen to you. I don't want to listen to *that*, all right. You know, Napoleon, *everything* doesn't have to do with *that*, does it? You're always talking about the same thing, no matter what anybody else is talking about."

"What?" he said, and he laughed when he said it. But he didn't think it was a bit funny. "Listen to you. Always talking about *that*? You can't even speak it. You can't even say what *that* is."

"Yes I can."

"No, you cannot."

I breathed a couple of loud, exasperated, steamy whistly breaths through my nose. Then I said it. "Blackness," I said.

I knew why he was laughing now. I tried to hold my hard-guy face but it was a chore. I had heard myself, after all. I said the word in such a ridiculous stage whisper, like a three-year-old with a secret. It was the best argument I could have made for Napoleon's side of things.

"That doesn't prove anything," I said, giving up to a small laugh myself.

Anyhow, I had managed to make him laugh. No small task. I didn't want to mess with that just yet.

We were nearing the bus stop in the square, the stop where all the Ward 17s waited to get bused out of here.

"Right," said Napoleon. "Here is a good example. You read the papers—"

"Sports pages only," I quickly pointed out.

"Yes, well if you were not *hiding* in the sports pages you would know that this city is a place where a lot of people would do anything to keep from going to school with black people."

"Maybe, but—"

"Richard, you have to know that that means a great many of the people who wind up in a school like yours—"

"Ours—"

"*Yours.* You have to know that they are there because

of hate. Because somebody hates—"

"I don't have to know that. I don't have to—"

"Yo," came the call from the bus stop.

"What?" I answered Butchie. Naturally enough I figured he meant me. But no. Not this time.

"Yo," he said again.

Napoleon ignored him, held his head even higher than usual, and strode on.

"Yo, Mowgli," Butchie called, "you deaf, or ignorant?"

I winced.

Napoleon Charlie Ellis did a rapid veer maneuver across the street toward the stop. I followed quickly after him. "Come on," I said, "you don't have to pay any attention to this."

"*You* don't have to pay attention to it," Napoleon said. "I do."

Once more, as seemed to be happening more frequently, Napoleon was suddenly up close with Butchie. "I am neither hard of hearing nor ignorant," he said evenly. "That is not my name, and you know it is not my name."

"I just thought," Butchie said, smiling, "that that's what your papa said he called you."

This was really, really close. I had never seen somebody get as mad as Napoleon was now, without somebody swinging at somebody.

"My *father*," Napoleon answered, "never said any such thing."

Butchie half-turned to face his group, which included Jum McDonaugh, Redheaded Beverly, and a dozen or so other kids who were only half-listening before but were inching closer now.

"I am sorry," Butch said. "I thought that was you he was talking about, Mowgli Tommy Ellis. And you love soup. Mowglitommy soup."

He got a few laughs with that, but less because people thought it was funny and more because they figured they were supposed to laugh. With Butch that was the quickest and most sensible way to get through something sticky. It was wise.

Napoleon Charlie Ellis was not wise.

"Is that supposed to be an imitation of me? Or of my father?"

"What?" Butchie said, in the broadest, stupidest, most simpleton voice he could muster. "Mowglitommy soup? You mean, Mowglitommy?"

"Shut up, Butch," I said. "You sound like a jerk."

He just grinned at me, like a jerk.

"Do you take this bus, Mowgli?" Jum McDonaugh threw in. "I never seen you on this bus. You wouldn't be going our way, would you?"

"I do not have to take any—"

"Right, your bus would be going the other way, huh? Takes me an hour and a half to get home. Must take a real long time to get you bused home, huh? It's, ah, south, isn't it? *Long* way south. Let us know if you need any help getting home. We could help you out, *bust* you home good and quick. Any ol' day."

"Let's go, Napoleon," I said, gently tugging on the front of his jacket. He squirmed out of my grip.

"If you don't like it," Napoleon said, "maybe you should not take the bus a'tall."

Both Jum and Butchie laughed hard at the sound. "A'tall. Naht a'tall," Jum said.

"That is right," Napoleon went on, composed but still angry just the same. You had to know him to really be able to tell when he was angry. And I was just getting to know him. "Maybe you should go to school where you belong, and leave us alone."

I had never seen a face go as red as Butchie's face went then.

"Where we *belong*?" He was bearing down on Napoleon now, with a stare so intense, his eyes were crossing, bulging, and going pink with bloodshot all at once. "What," Butchie said, "do you know," Butchie said, "about where," he said, "I be-long?"

If this was a film with no sound, and if you had never seen a fight build up before, you would still know, this was a fight building up.

"Shut *up*," Redheaded Beverly said, yanking Butch's arm.

He stopped moving toward Napoleon and turned on Beverly with enough force that it was almost as if he was moving on her now. He shook out of her grip violently.

So it was my turn to put a grip on him, and my turn to have his hot breath up my nose. "What's this, like one of them mass hysterical things? You all goin' nuts at the same time?" He was looking at me mean, but I was all right. I could do this with Butchie, at least this far. But as I said, I wasn't really willing to test it much further. I stood.

"You're just embarrassing everybody, Butch," Beverly said. And true enough, all the others, including Jum, had sort of backed away from him. They were like most people, happy to make noise, in a crowd, but not much more than that.

Butch was different. Butch wanted more than that.

The others all made a serious show of watching for the bus instead, as it now came into view.

"Stop giving the Ward a bad name," said Beverly.

The bus was pulling up to the curb when Butch gave me the smallest little shove in my chest, enough to push me back about three inches. But as he did it he was looking at Napoleon. And talking to Beverly.

"Okay Bev, I'll stop embarrassing you. Let's get on our scummy bus back to our scummy neighborhood where we can be ignorant and nobody'll notice, huh?"

The bus doors opened, the 17s filed on. Except for Beverly. As Butchie stepped up, she stepped back, and away. "I'll catch the next one," she said just before the driver snapped the door shut.

Butchie really was a silent film this time, as he stood staring wide-eyed and openmouthed at us through the bus window at bold Beverly the traitor.

"What a goon," Beverly said, then paused. "Shall we walk, boys?"

We walked, Redheaded Beverly in between Napoleon and me.

"I think you just need to ignore it," I said when we'd gone a silent half-block up Centre Street.

"I think you need to not ignore it," Napoleon said quietly.

"No, I just think . . . It's not really about you personally, right? I mean they really don't like that long ride to school . . . you wouldn't . . . I wouldn't. Really, you can't blame them, entirely."

"Why can't you?"

"If you knew them, that's all. I know they sound like jerks, but . . . especially Jum, he's not like that . . . they just don't speak their minds real well."

"Butch does," Beverly said. "He speaks his mind very well. It's just that there's not much in there."

With the added weight of Beverly's brain it would be fairly ridiculous to argue that. "Okay. Butch. Butch can be, y'know . . . but if you take away Butch—"

"The problem remains," Napoleon said. This time he didn't sound like he was fighting. He sounded like he was despairing.

Napoleon simply shook his head, saying no more through the rest of the walk to the next bus stop where Beverly would be getting aboard for real. She looked at me. I shrugged and looked back. The bits of snow still lying around from last night's blanketing were turning to crunch by the minute as the temperature dropped.

"It is so cold here," Napoleon finally said.

"It will warm up eventually," I said. "You learn not to feel the cold so much. Just like you learn not to be so stubborn, and not to listen to stuff. You'll learn."

"I will not," he said firmly.

"I don't want to talk about them anymore," Beverly said. "The real reason I didn't take the early bus even though I'm *freezing* my toes off, is I wanted to tell you that I think your father is incredible, Napoleon. He's a real artist. And a performer."

Napoleon looked at his feet.

"And really handsome," she added.

Napoleon looked up. So did I.

"You must be very proud," Beverly said.

"I must be," he answered, and I believed I could see the first evidence of bashfulness out of Napoleon Charlie Ellis. He was always kind of reserved, but it was never the same as shyness or anything like that.

I liked it.

"Didn't know you could be bashful," I said.

"I am not," he said, to his feet again.

"Leave him alone," Beverly said, laughing a bit. She shoved me off the curb. "I bet you'd be bashful too, if anybody ever had a reason to compliment *you*."

I got back up to the curb. "I'm full of a lot of things, but bash ain't one of 'em," I said, and shoved her this time, into Napoleon.

He barely reacted, even though Redheaded Beverly

knocked him off his straight and narrow and he had to have noticed since he was watching his feet so closely. He did manage a smile, though, even if he did try not to share it.

"My bus is coming," Beverly said. "But also, I wanted to ask, are we on for this Saturday?"

Napoleon Charlie Ellis and Richard Riley Moncreif answered simultaneously.

"On *what*?" said I.

"Certainly," said he.

He and I looked at each other while Beverly enlightened us. "The youth symphony. It's this Saturday morning, and you said you would go. Remember the bet?"

Rats, I thought. But I had to do better than that.

"Can't. Napoleon and I have the batting cage booked for then."

"We can cancel that," he said. "The symphony would be grand."

"*Grand?*"

"Cool," Beverly said. "It's at ten."

The bus was almost there. She stepped off the curb.

"Beverlyyy," I whined.

"You gave your word," she said.

"So give it back," I said.

She waved me off, disgusted. "If you really don't want to go, Richard, I'm not going to force you. That would be pointless."

"Dynamite," I said. "Thanks, you're a sport, Bev. Tell us all about it on Monday."

"We will," Napoleon said slyly.

"Dynamite!" Beverly said as she jumped on the bus.

I was so dumbfounded all I could do was stutter and splutter at him. "Wha . . . baseball, Nappp . . . we were suppp . . . you can't just . . ."

Napoleon's mood had gone up several notches, and it was his turn to try and pull me through a rough spot. He did a bad job of it, though.

"There will be other days, Richard," he said with his hand on my shoulder. "It is only baseball, after all."

"*Only* . . . baseball? Only *baseball*? Man, have you been listening to *anything* I've been trying to teach you?"

His seriousness came back. At least the appearance of seriousness. "Yes, Richard, I have been listening. But a lot of it . . . a lot of it is *nonsense*."

For somebody so polite, he was getting pretty free with knocking *me* around.

We were just about to go our own ways, but I had to make the point. "So, symphony with Beverly on Saturday morning and dinner with me on Saturday night. See? Who says you're hopeless? Just imagine how many friends you'd have if you made a little *effort* to get along with people?"

He shook his head. "Get along," he said, brushing me off.

WINTER
HAVEN

Saturday morning. I was up, as planned, bright and early to get my cuts in. They had the nets strung up all over the humongous Northeastern University gym, for their ballplayers to get in their first work of the season. I was already weeks ahead of them, so it was only right that I should have the place to myself first.

The custodian was good about it as long as you didn't crank up the machine. His idea of cranking up the machine was getting it to throw pitches hard enough to bruise a banana.

But I didn't mind. A slow groove was fine enough with me. It was, after all, mighty cold outside, even for me, and my hands would hold up longer over the season if I didn't freeze them into splinters in spring training.

And there was another reason the slower pace suited me. Fred Lynn.

Fred Lynn.

He was almost here. I could just about smell him.

I had heard about him as far back as his college days at USC. Followed him to the minor leagues, even caught a few glimpses of him on the sportcenter end of the six o'clock news, which will tell you something right there since almost nobody in this town cares enough to look at some kid who might come to the Sox two years from now. Not with the Bruins and the Celtics and once in a while even the Patriots playing big-time major league sports right now.

So I'd been patiently paying my dues, waiting, hearing about him coming around the corner for a while now like he was the bingling music of the ice-cream man a block away on the hottest day of the year. I even went and joined the Boy Scouts for a week in the spring of 1974 because I heard they were making a trip to Pawtucket to see the triple-A farm team with Fred Lynn on it. I went on that trip, and it didn't matter whether Fred Lynn was hitting or roaming around center field or drinking lemonade in the home dugout of McCoy Stadium, I could not take my eyes off him.

Because he did it all so well. Every stride, every stretch, every gesture, every stroke, he did like nobody I had ever seen before. He did it like he was supposed to be doing it, like he was never supposed to leave the field because he was built purely for baseball and baseball was built purely for him. We had been waiting for Fred Lynn forever. At least I had been. I know a lot of people felt that way, and I know a lot of people thought he was special, but I refuse to believe anyone felt it like I felt it and there is one more thing I was sure of that day at McCoy Stadium in Pawtucket, Rhode Island, at the end of my one and only week as a Boy Scout of America.

I was sure that, while I could not take my eyes off of Fred Lynn, he was watching me as well.

That is true. Time, after time, after time, when I stared down on Fred Lynn so hard you'd think he would have felt the heat of my vision burning holes in his Pawsox cap, it turned out he felt it indeed. For no apparent reason he would stop looking at the batter from center field, stop sizing up the pitcher from the batter's box, and he would look right at me.

How many people can say that? If anybody else says it was them he was looking at, they are imagining it.

And then, finally, there he was. February 1975, there he was with the rest of the Sox in Winter Haven. He was doing his thing and doing it on the major league diamond, not with all the kids who were going to play maybe next year or the year after. Fred Lynn was with us, and was never going to be leaving us again.

And I had to be him. There was nothing else to be. Everyone was going to want to be Fred Lynn eventually, I was certain of that. Of course they were. Who wouldn't? But he was mine. I had believed before anyone. So when there was the big rush to be Fred Lynn, it was only right that I would be Fred Lynn first. Well, second anyway.

His instincts were perfect. When he ran, he did not

blow you away with his speed, but at the same time he appeared to reach every ball hit catchably to center field. He could not have covered more ground in less time if he had somebody driving him, and he didn't run to greet the ball so much as he glided. He never ran the wrong way when he heard the pop of the ball off the bat, and if the hit reached the warning track or was going over the wall into the bull pen, he would time his leap perfectly and never, ever, lose a ball once he got a glove on it.

Even more than saving home runs, though, I loved to watch him come in on a short ball. As if he was somehow doing the calculations of time and distance and trajectory and drop in his head while at the same time running just like a kid who was doing it for plain fun instead of for his profession, Fred Lynn was always arriving to the spot where the ball was trying to get to the ground just in time to stop it from getting there. Flopping and sliding and tumbling all over the place, he still never seemed like he was out of control or one inch off the mark. I swore if he closed his eyes and ran straight ahead he would still wind up with the ball in his glove. And the perfect grass of the Fenway outfield would cradle him like a baby. The finest field in baseball, groundskeeper Joe Mooney's Fenway lawn. Finest field in the world.

That world now belonged to Fred Lynn. He controlled it totally.

But the stroke was the thing. It was the most perfect and beautiful thing I had ever seen. I know that other people, like Beverly, can hear it in music. I can't hear music. Some people see what I'm talking about in ballet, or in the shapes of sculpture.

But I don't see that. I see it, and believe that I see somehow everything that is good and right and important, in a flawless, speedy and powerful swing of a baseball bat in pursuit of a ball.

And I never saw it perfect until I saw Fred Lynn. God gave it all to Fred Lynn.

And he gave Fred Lynn to me.

And I was going to repay him by learning to be great myself. Which was going to require some work. Beginning with the small job of turning myself from a right-handed hitter into a left-handed hitter. I was only half kidding about that. I would in time go back to the right side because I was already too far along. But I felt like I could understand what Lynn did better, I could get him *down*, if I did it by the numbers. By his numbers. I wanted to be over there, in his shoes, and *feel* it.

It felt funny. Strange at first, but not entirely foreign. I had taken a few cuts from the left side before because if you truly want to be the best hitter you can be you have to at least briefly toy with the idea of being a switch hitter. I toyed with it very briefly. Because I ran out of patience quickly when I realized it wasn't nearly as fun working from the other side. I did okay as a lefty, but I couldn't smack the ball the way I was used to and if I couldn't smack it then I got frustrated, and if I got frustrated I pressed too hard and if I pressed too hard I lost control and hit worse and worse little squibbly nothings. Then I would jump over to the right side, crank a few shots, sigh and smile and never want to leave that box again because the right box was the right box, and I was right when I was in it, and Jeez, why should you have to work twice as hard for something if you don't have to.

I was younger then. That was before I could see very far into the future. That was before Fred Lynn was sent to me to show me.

So the slow pitch machine was fine for the time being. I dug in my feet, rubbed my right hand all the way up to the end of the bat like Fred did, and calmly sat back waiting for what came.

Pop, not bad. *Smack*, better. I could do this. *Smack* again, I was going with the pitches, just the way Fred was doing in Winter Haven as he prepared to use Fenway's Green Monster left field wall. I couldn't muscle anything yet, but I could use what the machine gave me, take what I could get, take advantage. Control I would learn first, and power would follow, as I was certain Fred himself had learned.

But what I did not like. What I did not like was the way, for the first time in a long time, I did not feel right with a baseball bat in my hands. I did not feel, instinctively, that I was where I belonged. I did not know without question that I was doing what god and the world and Fred Lynn wanted me to do and it made me weirdly, dizzily, and scarily, nervous. Like I was in the wrong body, in the wrong place, doing the wrong thing. Like I did not now understand the world, where I could have sworn I completely understood it a few minutes before.

This could not be allowed. I took a step off the plate and rested the head of the bat on the ground. I closed my eyes and remembered what I wanted. I remembered that baseball would only get better if I learned it better from all angles. I wanted that. Of course I wanted that. I would master this, I would control it. And I would love it even more.

It was going to take a hard head, though.

I stepped back in.

There were a lot of awful swings to get out of my system, and there was nobody there to take it out on when the whole deal made me angry. All there was to do was to keep on doing. Steady. Steady. I could do this.

I took pitch after pitch after pitch, as if to show the pitching machine that it was going to break down before I would. When it ran out of balls I ran to refill it.

Gradually, it came. I'd swing, I'd make contact, I'd recoil into my well-practiced mini-Lynn stance, and I'd snap out at it again. The ball came, I sent it back. The ball came, I sent it back. I was every bit as oiled as the machine that was pitching to me, and after a while just as unconscious of it. The groove I slipped into must have been the thing I had heard long-distance runners talk about, a kind of trance thing that feels like a whole nother kind of life.

Because by the time the machine had emptied once more and sat there just humming at me, wanting to throw something at me but having nothing left, the college guys were already gathering around at the sides, and I never even noticed them coming in. I didn't even stop hovering over the plate waiting on the next pitch that wasn't coming, until several of them started clapping for me.

They must have been watching for a while. I felt flushed, embarrassed and proud, but most of all, exposed. I never think of anybody watching me when I'm hitting, because I'm thinking about . . . hitting. Especially when I had to work so hard at it.

These were baseball guys, though. Not just players, but *players*. Felt kind of nice, the few splashes of applause. From people who appreciated.

I have always sort of assumed nobody properly could. Appreciate it.

I gave them a short little wave, scooped up my jacket and gloves. I pulled my Bruins ski cap down low, put my Adirondack on my shoulder and hurried on out.

I was standing there on Huntington Avenue, crusted snow under my sneakers, and fresh stuff dropping out of the sky in fat wet flakes that were going to put off real outdoor spring ball just a little bit longer. That only meant that it would be harder to get other guys to play with me, not that I wouldn't do it myself. But once I taught Napoleon, once I showed him baseball the way I loved baseball. . . . I was starting to feel like he might be the one.

The one hardheaded enough to go the route with me. The one guy who, when I turned around on a bitter November afternoon, would possibly be standing there, ready to throw.

You can be better, probably, if somebody pushes you, and that was Napoleon Charlie Ellis. He was a lot of things I had never met before.

I could see us in February, and March, and next February and March, taking turns throwing live batting practice to each other while the other guys sat rusting and getting fat before the season. And that with each season we would leave them all further and further behind on our way to being better, and better, and best.

Like Fred Lynn and Jim Rice. The Gold Dust Twins. We could do that. We could *outdo* that.

My heart was pounding.

Except my twin was wasting away over in Symphony Hall, which . . . was only a block away. I felt I had a duty.

When I got there, the snow was falling heavily, and I took shelter under the big awning in front of the main entrance. "How long before the concert gets out?" I asked the white-haired doorman.

He looked at his watch. "I don't know," he said.

There were several doors, each with its own one of those guys in their red coats, sitting on little wooden stools. I tried the next one. "What time does it let out?" I asked.

He looked at my bat. "What do you plan to do with that, kid?"

I looked at my bat. I had forgotten it was there, up on my shoulder. I shrugged, and watched it move while I shrugged. "Play baseball?"

"Get outta here, ya loon, and stop pullin' my chain."

Door number three. This guy didn't have white hair, because he had no hair. And he had a thin white wire running from the inside breast pocket of that red jacket to his ear. He had a look of concentration fixed on his face as he stared off into what looked like nowhere, except I know better. Enough teachers have caught me doing the same thing.

With a start he caught sight of me coming up beside him and after catching his breath and a look at the Adirondack half frosted in snow, he smiled and tugged the earpiece out of his large fleshy pink ear.

He reached out and stuck the earpiece in my own ear, nudging my cap up to get under there. It was Red Sox–Tigers. Grapefruit League from Florida.

He took my bat, gripping it, weighing it, checking the balance. He pulled the wire out of my ear. "February hitter, huh?"

I shrugged. It felt a little like confession.

He was still balancing the bat, looking at it as he talked.

"That kid Lynn, huh. . . ." he said, rubbing a thumb up and down over the grain.

"Ya," I said.

The man handed me back my bat. "You know, you

don't have to turn the label around toward the back when you're hittin'. That's just a myth."

"Really?"

"Ya, the bat won't break. Unless you hit it wrong to begin with. Then it don't matter if you got the label in your back pocket, the thing'll break. But you'll be all right, huh? You studyin'?"

I nodded again.

He nodded back. "I was gonna be Ted Williams. Teddy Ballgame. You know Ted, o'course."

I knew Ted, like everybody who knew anything around here knew Ted. He was a legendary figure, still made the news when he showed up as a roving instructor at Winter Haven. Set a lot of records, took off the best four years of his career to be a pilot in World War Two, then came back and did great again. Hit a home run in his very last at-bat. I knew Ted Williams. But he was no Fred Lynn.

I whispered. I felt stupid saying it out loud, about telling the world, but not about telling this man. "I'm gonna be Fred Lynn."

"I know," he said. "You waiting on somebody? Get on in here, and wait in the lobby. Get them hands out of the February."

So I did. I got to kind of wander around in the warm, red-carpeted lobby, and off in the distance, I could hear the big sound of the orchestra playing something I actually thought I recognized. Why? I had no business recognizing anything in there.

Except. Right, the Esplanade on the Fourth of July. Every Fourth, after watching the Sox beat somebody in the afternoon, practically the whole city listens to the Pops orchestra play this very tune as the fireworks blast off. The 1812 Overture. It's good, it has cannons. But there was no way the rest of the show could have matched it.

And then it was over, and I waited. Kids and kids and kids started piling out of the auditorium, into the lobby, out of the lobby, and onto Mass. Ave. There must have been seating for a million in that place because not only could I not see Napoleon and Red-headed Beverly, I couldn't really make out any faces at all. It was like a sea of faces, and they all looked pretty much the same, pale and bombed-out and focused on the snow that was coming down hard out there.

I just kept looking, and looking, going high up on my toes, then scrunching down low like a nut, as if I could find them *under* the throng. The crowd was getting thinner, and I still was getting nowhere, and may have even missed them already. Finally, I took off my Bruins hat and put it up on the end of my bat, and held the bat high in the air. If *that* didn't stand as my own personal flag, nothing would. If I got the chance to hit the moon with the next Apollo mission, that was what I would stick in the moon dirt so all my friends would know it was me.

But this was not the moon, even if the symphony was pretty close.

"What are you doing, kid? Go on, get outta here," one of the white-haired doormen said. The nice guy, the baseball guy, stepped in and told me I could stay, but I wanted to go by now anyway. The last stragglers were filing out. I had missed my chance.

"You know what I would do in weather like this," the baseball guy said. "I would go over to the Christian Science Center. Pack a stack of hard iceballs, then hit 'em out of my hand. I used to do that down the field for hours and hours, in the winters when I couldn't get nobody to play with me. And the Christian Science Center is the closest thing to a field. In snow can't tell the difference, right?"

"You are really crazy, Richard, you know that?"

I looked up to see the very last two symphoniacs, or whatever their kind are called, stepping gently down the stairs. It was Beverly doing the talking, but Napoleon Charlie Ellis was grinning pretty hard.

All at once it hit me, as they took the steps in sync, graceful as a couple of movie musical dancers, and as close as a wedding couple.

There they were. They were a they.

So? So. That didn't bother me. Why should that bother me?

"I'm not crazy," I said, finally thinking to remove my Bruins cap from the end of the bat.

"Was its little head getting cold?" Beverly said, patting the top of my bat.

They were all dressed up, as if it was nighttime and

they were forced by their parents to do something boring and awful. Only nobody was forcing them. It made less and less sense. Napoleon was wearing a long navy blue wool overcoat, black leather gloves, and new-looking shiny black galoshes. Beverly had on a coat of similar length and material, only red, with a kind of lamby collar and a matching hat.

They were such a *they*. How and when had that happened, and exactly what, I was asking myself, what business was it of mine? They looked good, like a shrunk-down dressed-up pair of fancy classical music adults, or a pair of pumped-up plastic dolls off a wedding cake. And anyway, why even notice?

Because it felt like somebody was stealing from me. Who, stealing what? I had no idea. Stupid. I felt angry. No, no, just stupid. I was out of my element, was the thing. I really needed to get back where I belonged.

"What are you doing here?" Napoleon asked.

"I came to rescue *you*," I said, pointing at him.

"From what?" Beverly asked. "From culture? From music? From civilization, pleasure, *me*?"

I stared dumbly at her. "Yes," I finally said. "Come on, Napoleon, you served your sentence, now I'm here to spring you."

"You do not know what you missed," he said to me. "You really should have come."

"Really," Beverly agreed, "it was marvelous. Even you would have appreciated it."

The "even you" bit didn't even bother me. "Ya, well,

you don't know what *you* missed. All I did was teach myself to be Fred Lynn, over there at Northeastern, that's all. And if you're gonna be Jim Rice with me we have a lot of work to do starting right away."

He closed his eyes and shook his head. "Is that who we are going to be? Can't we be who we already are?"

Beverly put a hand lightly on Napoleon's hand. My eyes went to it like a laser. "If he's this worked up, they must be pretty decent baseball players."

"These are not *just* decent baseball players. This is Lynn and Rice. The best pair of rookies, ever. The Gold Dust Twins . . ."

"Well that is interesting, if they are twins. I didn't even know they were related."

"No, not actually . . . come on, Napoleon. I'll explain it while we're, you know, while . . ." Somewhere in there I must have suspected the baseball-in-a-blizzard idea was not quite all there, if I couldn't even speak it.

But it didn't change my mind.

"Tell me you're not here to force poor Napoleon to play baseball in this? Tell me that, Richard."

"I . . . I'd like to tell you that. . . ."

"Nut," she said, but she didn't say it the way a lot of people would.

"The Gold Dust Twins," I said again to Napoleon. "I just had this thought . . . all right, there is a possibility that this will sound a little nutty . . . anyway . . . you can hit, I can tell that already. I just feel like . . . that could be us."

As the words came out, I felt as if the ground had

been whipped out from under me. I was hanging there, floating and exposed in the snow. I looked away.

If Napoleon thought I was a nut he was doing a very kind job of not letting me know. "I don't have much of an idea of what you are talking about, Richard."

I was feeling really foolish now, at the symphony, during a snowstorm, blurting out my mental vision that now was starting to sound like nonsense even to me because the air of the real world was now all over it.

"Nevermind," I said.

"No," he said. "I like the sound of it anyway, Gold Dust Twins." He nodded, looking out at the sky where you couldn't see a thing. Flakes of snow settled on his face, and melted there, leaving small shining dots.

"Oh you're not seriously . . ." Redheaded Beverly was openly laughing at the two of us now.

"Do you mind if I go?" he said to her.

"Well, I don't suppose even baseball—even snow baseball—can undo what the symphony does for a person. But you still owe me a trip to Brigham's."

Now it was Napoleon's turn to shake his head at her. "I cannot understand why you people up here are so interested in ice cream in this weather."

Beverly gave Napoleon a mysterious grin, pulled her collar tight around her neck, and headed off through the snow, humming loudly some classical something that did not have cannons in it.

"So," Napoleon said, producing from his pocket his

black Bruins cap and pulling it low over his ears. "This had better be good."

My man. I knew it. My snowstorm-baseball-hardhead partner.

"I knew I was right about you," I said.

He shrugged.

I handed him my Adirondack and started towing him along by it. "I'll pitch you snowballs. This is excellent quality snowball snow. I know this great great place, the Christian Science Center—been there?—and anyway, you're gonna love it, trust me, you are gonna love this, I know you are."

"Fine. And then, I will teach you cricket, and you will love that. Trust me, I know you will."

"Oh, well, ya, sure, we'll see . . . y'know, take it one step at a time, right?" I knew once I showed him baseball, the way I knew baseball, that the cricket stuff just wouldn't be an issue anymore. I just knew this, inside.

But I also knew that at this moment he didn't care one lick about baseball. And he was coming with me anyway. *That* was something.

Behind me, Napoleon Charlie Ellis was laughing. Which I figured meant he was aware of it too.

He stopped walking and flattened out his feet, letting me pull him like a sled to the snowfield. Which I was happy to do.

FOREIGN
TERRITORY

Frozen hours is what they were, the time Napoleon and I spent on the tundra of the Christian Science Center. I would lob my perfectly sculpted ice balls after stacking them in a neat pyramid by my side like cannonballs. Easy at first, but after Napoleon had loosened up—he was out there in his Symphony Geek outfit after all—I could see that it would do no harm at all to throw him harder, then harder stuff. The extra speed, the extra motion of it all was good for both of us, not just because it was a lot more fun—which it was—but also because it helped us to stave off death. It was *cold* out there.

Which Napoleon had to be feeling even more than I did. But you'd never know it. He stood in there, taking his cuts, blowing on his hands, taking his cuts, missing a lot of pitches but now and then catching one and smashing it to smithereens so spectacularly that we had to try and do it again even before all the hundred million little crystals had landed back on earth again.

In fact, we got it going so well, I didn't even take a turn hitting.

I said, I didn't even take a turn hitting.

I was more regular than the pitching machine in the cage, cranking and cranking, until my gloves got so wet and frosty it was warmer to throw them off. Napoleon, for his part, was taking one mean cut after another even though I could see, after a while, that he was slowing down and stiffening up, in his leather-gloved hands, his wool-jacketed arms.

Finally I just stopped pitching and walked up to him. He stood there, as if waiting for the next pitch, as if he was a statue and couldn't even tell that I was walking up close. Only then, two feet away, could I really tell how cold he was. His lips were a very unusual and couldn't-possibly-be-healthy shade of purply charcoal. His grip on the bat was so hard it was like one of those guys who get themselves stuck to a frozen sign pole by licking it.

"You want to quit?" I asked.

He didn't even answer.

"Hello? Hey, are you all right?" I patted his shoulder, mostly to test if anyone was still in there.

Even his voice was frozen. "We . . . can . . . continue . . . for . . . a . . . while . . . if . . . you . . ."

I was afraid if I waited for him to finish he might not survive. "You better get home before you die," I said.

He nodded, and did not struggle as I removed the bat from his hands.

"Anyone ever tell you you were kind of stubborn?"

"N-no," he stammered.

I shook my head.

It occurred to me as we shuffled across the broad snow plain that I had never before seen a person so far out of his element.

That is, until we got me to Anthony's Pier 4 Restaurant.

The very idea of me going to a fancy restaurant was so out of the normal that this is how it went when I left the house, calling back over my shoulder from the front porch:

"See ya, I'm going out to Anthony's Pier Four with the new kid in school and his father who's a university professor."

"Hey," my father barked from the living room. If you knew my house, I would not have had to add the part about barking from the living room. If he speaks, odds are pretty strong he is barking from the living room. "Young man, you are not going anywhere unless you tell me where you are really going."

The Pier 4 idea was not even a possibility.

"Movies," I said.

"Be back by ten," he said.

"Okay," I said.

I could be back by midnight if I wanted, since by ten

he was always asleep. In the living room.

I had told Napoleon that he and his dad could pick me up on the corner in front of Woolworth's. I said it was because my steep narrow hill was rotten in the winter with the ice and with cars parked all the way on both sides up and down making it more likely than not that someone not used to it would have an accident. Which was true. If it was summer, I would have had to think of something else, though.

"Well, Richard," Dr. Ellis said when we had been seated by a guy in a suit who made me feel like I ought to have been serving him. "We are very pleased you could make it this evening. Aren't we, son?"

"Yes," Napoleon said. "Thank you, Richard."

You might have thought that was the kind of thing a guy was saying because his father was forcing him to, but I could believe him. He sounded sincere. And he had already thanked me about three times in the car.

"Happy to be here," I said.

A guy in a white suit came by then and served us these giant, mushroom-shaped rolls with big tongs. We hadn't even ordered any.

"This is cool," I said. "Nice place."

"You have never been here before," Dr. Ellis said.

I shook my head. "We eat at home pretty much all the time. I do the cooking a lot even. So this is a treat."

"How many of you are at home then?" the doctor asked.

Oh no. How was I getting into this? I thought we were going to be talking about baseball. Even Caribbean literature would be better than this. Like I said, the way things went there wasn't a great need to talk about yourself or your home very much. You just figured everyone was aware of everyone and kind of shut up about it. I liked it that way.

"Just the two of us, sir," I said. "Me and my dad."

"Like us," Napoleon said, as if we were all a part of this excellent club.

"Ya," I said, looking at the two of them all dusted up and starched and looking like one of those Father's Day sale ads for Filene's. Napoleon had to be the only guy in the world who got *more* dressed up after he took off the school uniform every afternoon.

"Oh my, I wish I had known that," Dr. Ellis said. "We could have asked your father along."

Yikes.

"He doesn't like restaurants much. Kind of . . . kind of a homebody."

"What does he do for work?"

"He works for Midas. You know, the muffler guys?"

"Ah, yes," he said, and looked at me then with what felt like was a little extra X ray. As if he was trying to figure out how far to go with these questions. He paused. "So, you are a huge baseball fan."

Dr. Ellis was a good man. A very good, polite man.

Trying to be likewise, I made every effort to discuss

baseball without being boring, or nuts. Mostly I talked about the league I played in, the Sox games I'd seen, and about us, me and Napoleon.

"Should have seen him today, sir. Napoleon was tearing the ball up."

"Yes," Dr. Ellis said, grinning as he half-buried his face in the gigantic laminated menu. "I spent most of the afternoon bringing him large cups of tea and keeping the fireplace tended."

I looked at Napoleon, who looked at his menu. "It wasn't *most* of the afternoon," he grumbled.

I made a pass at joining in the menu reading. But very quickly I got overwhelmed. There had to be thirty different things on the menu, and that was just the appetizer page. And an appetizer cost more than we usually spent on the makings of a whole meal at home.

I tried to remain cool. I tried not to turn red, but I felt it happening to me anyway. The lights from the chandeliers were getting hotter and hotter. I took a long drink of water, and as soon as I put my glass down some other white-shirt guy was there bang on the spot to refill me. I practically shrank from him. I did not like service, I decided.

I started thinking of how I was going to repay Dr. Ellis. Shovel his driveway. For two years. Have my father realign his brakes—I glanced again at the menu—and throw in a couple of new tires.

I closed the menu.

"Ah, decided already," Dr. Ellis said.

No, panicked, actually. But I kept quiet.

"Are you having the swordfish?" Napoleon asked.

"Ha-ha," I said.

Next thing I knew, Dr. Ellis was ordering from the fancy waiter. Ordering quickly. Ordering what sounded like a lot. In what sounded like French.

I must have been staring.

"In addition to Caribbean literature, he is an instructor in the French department simultaneously," Napoleon informed me.

This was getting pretty heady for me. I drained my water. It was refilled. The French department. My father's idea of accomplishing two things simultaneously is having a drink in the shower. Normally, I think that's pretty cool myself, but it doesn't give me a lot to talk about at times like this. I hate times like this.

What was I doing here? Napoleon and his dad were so easy with everything, so smooth and natural. I was like . . . fish out of water doesn't even cover it. I was embarrassed. Ashamed, like I had done something when I hadn't done anything. And guilty for even *being* there.

Napoleon ordered. In French.

"I'll have the chicken," I said.

This, apparently, would not do.

"Sir," the waiter asked, pointing at a section of the menu that took up roughly the same space as the Soviet Union on the classroom wall map. "Which chicken would that be?"

I pointed blindly. "That one, please."

It might not have fooled anybody, but it did the job. The waiter left. And left me with the Ellis family. I was sure they must by now be dying of embarrassment at the scrub they brought with them to dinner.

"We were talking about baseball," Napoleon said, rescuing me.

"Yes," his father said. "Tell me, Richard, are you aware of this fellow Jim Rice? I hear talk around campus that he is supposed to be quite a phenomenon. Then I saw him on the news report the other evening, and indeed he appears to be something special. But you must be aware of him, I'm sure."

"Well . . . sure, he is. Rice is going to be great," I said. "But, you know, really, the big story is Fred Lynn. They must be talking about Fred Lynn, around the campus?"

Napoleon cut in. "What do you know about baseball, Father? You don't follow baseball."

"I know enough. I played some baseball in my day. It is a fine sport, and I am glad to see you getting involved in it."

"He is, sir," I said. "Getting real involved in it. People are starting to call us the Gold Dust Twins, you know, like Fred Lynn and Jim Rice. You know Fred Lynn, don't you, Dr. Ellis?"

"What?" Napoleon said. "People are calling us that? What people are calling us that?"

"I think that is wonderful, the two of you are getting renowned for your ability. Is that what they call these two players? The Gold Dust Twins? That is marvelous."

One of the waiters set a bowl of creamy soup in front of Dr. Ellis. It reeked of fish.

"What people are calling us the Gold Dust Twins?" Napoleon demanded. "I am sure they are calling us something, but I highly doubt that is it."

Dr. Ellis sipped the soup and declared it "beauteous. Would anyone care to taste?" We declined. "So tell me more. Is this fellow Lynn as good as the man Rice?"

"Oh ya," I said. "Rice is really really good, but Fred Lynn is even better. But together they are going to be awesome."

"Like the two of you," Dr. Ellis said between mouthfuls. "Bravo."

He appeared to be truly happy about this. Napoleon was more serious, more hung up on details. "No one is really calling us the Gold Dust Twins, are they?"

I busied myself pulling apart my roll, which was hard and crackly on the outside and kind of slick and hollow on the inside. This might have been a fancy place, but they could learn a thing from Wonder bread.

"Richard?"

"All right, *I* call us that. But you watch, pretty soon others will follow."

"And I will," Dr. Ellis said, smiling. "The Gold Dust Twins. I am having dinner with the Gold Dust Twins."

"See," I said to Napoleon. "Feels good, don't it?"

Napoleon had his own roll popped open and his head down, as if he was trying to fit his face inside the mushroom-cap top half of it. "No, it does not. It feels rather silly at the moment."

Dr. Ellis had just finished his soup and as if on command, a team of waiters came with the main dishes. I had apparently ordered my chicken with some kind of tan-colored sauce with mushrooms thrown all over the place, and like five different vegetables, three of which I had never seen before. And they came on their own separate plate.

Napoleon had something on his plate that looked like a steak but wasn't fooling anyone. That was a fish.

Dr. Ellis had lobster. It looked like lobster.

"Did you know," Dr. Ellis said, "that there is a great pitcher called Doc Ellis. He pitches for Pittsburgh, I think. Doc Ellis. Isn't that something?"

"Yes," I said. "He is great. He pitched a no-hitter one time, and he even did it while he was on drugs."

"Oh," Dr. Ellis said, a little flat.

Napoleon glared at me.

"I'm sorry," I said, and I was. I hadn't meant to be insulting. "Is he a relative?"

Napoleon glared at me.

"What?" I said. I didn't know, but I apologized again anyway. I didn't know how to do this. I was well aware I didn't know how to act right. Even talking baseball didn't seem safe, which was about as serious a warning sign as I could get. I worked up a fine sweat trying to eat my food just right, using all the utensils they had given me even though they had given me enough to work a whole farm with. I watched the Ellises, imitated them as much as possible while still checking the crowd and the staff and my shirtfront to make sure I had not made any spectacular errors.

It was hard work. Supper shouldn't be hard work. Meeting and talking and eating with people should not be hard work. But then again, I should remember it could always be harder.

"We really should think about getting together, the four of us, some night," Dr. Ellis said as we neared the end of the meal. He was very neatly working his way through a strawberry shortcake with such style that he was never once in danger of a drip. "Do consider mentioning it to your father, would you, Richard?"

I had all my attention focused on monitoring my cheesecake. "I sure will, sir. Thank you, I will mention it."

"Great," Napoleon said.

I don't know if he was joking, or if he really believed I would do it.

You don't have to know everything in the world to get by. Because there are a few things that, if you know them, they cover a lot of the others. Your limits, like. Your strengths and soft spots and shouldn't-go-theres. Like if the pitcher has a killer sinkerball, don't try and hit it. Wait for your pitch.

This was not my dad's pitch. Me and my dad are great. I like him fine. He's mine. You have to like your people, I think, because they're yours. Other folks don't have to like them.

I didn't think the Ellises would like my dad a lot. And I didn't think he'd like them a lot.

The ride home, through light sparkly crystal snowfall, was nice. It's always nice, with a full belly, walking out into the cold but then climbing into a plush and warm car instead of a rattly, drafty rust box with dodgy heat. Half-sleepy dreamy during the trip, I was relaxed and grateful, listening more than talking with the Ellises—which was a good thing. Snowflakes caught in streetlights became baseballs hit into the dark skies of night games, one after another disappearing over the wall. Napoleon sat next to me in the backseat, looking likewise outside but maybe thinking entirely different things, I couldn't tell. Snow was still kind of foreign to him.

"Right here," I said, as Dr. Ellis was about to pass right by Woolworth's. "The driving will be ten times worse now, even, with this new snow."

As I opened my door, Dr. Ellis reached over the back-seat, and shook my hand, thanking me.

A shock ran through me, from my hand on up through my whole upper body. Thanking *me*. Thanking me?

It was a great, firm, and honest handshake.

Then I reached over and shook Napoleon's. Seemed like the thing to do.

Same. Firm, honest handshake.

"See you Monday," I said.

"See you Monday."

I stood on the corner waving, seeing them off, until I saw them gone.

And headed up my hill.

NOT
CRICKET

Monday was gorgeous. One of the great things about being in Boston was that, just as soon as you got the feeling in January or February or March that the weather was brutal and would remain brutal for the rest of your life—a feeling you could get pretty frequently in January or February or March—then bang came a day to make you walk around with wow in your stomach and a mad itch in your feet. To get out there and play a game.

Which we did at lunchtime. Every kid in the school was climbing over every other kid to get through the door, still chewing, still slurping, bits of ham or apple or jelly falling down our shirts as we rushed the exit.

There was no doubt what I was intending to do. Not on a midwinter day when it was nearly sixty degrees and the sun was throwing brightness over everything. My dream, a dream I had over and over again during the previous three hours while the teachers were probably discussing math or god or poetry, involved swinging some sort of stick at some sort of sphere.

"You know what's been running through my head all morning, Napoleon?" I asked as we scooted across the asphalt toward the back of the Sisters' four-car garage. That was where the odd old broom handles were stashed, and we all knew what odd old broom handles were good for, so you had to get there early or lose out.

Napoleon snorted. "The whole world knows what has been running through your head all morning. Baseball has been running through your head all morning."

"Well, ya, of course, but I don't even have to say that. I mean, along *with* baseball."

"Apparently there is a great deal of room up there," he said, reaching over and tapping the side of my head. Like he expected an echo.

"Because I am in such a good mood," I said, picking up the first thick, strong broom handle, "I won't even mind that you did that. And I will tell you that what has been running through my head is the theme to *Hawaii Five-O*."

I was very serious, and very excited.

"I'm holding a big stick, Napoleon. You better cut that out."

He was laughing.

"You mean the theme music. From that television program with the police officer with the metal hairstyle."

"That's not the point," I snapped. "It's the music, the *sound*." I jumped into my batting stance, and began my rendition of the surfy, coppy song—Ba-ba-ba-ba-BAH-ba, ba-ba-ba-ba-baaaaa—swinging my bat as hard as I could in either direction every other beat. "It's the perfect baseball soundtrack, and I was brilliant on the field all morning. In my head."

I could not stop moving as I talked, and Napoleon could not stop smiling. It was the kind of thing that I knew was contagious, and that I knew all along he would eventually catch from me. And then we would be off into history, the Gold Dust Twins.

In truth, I wasn't the only one with the fever. Various strains were happening all over the schoolyard. There was mad motion in every direction and even the yard monitors, Sister Esther and Sister Margaret, couldn't seem to keep from grinning as they patrolled the grounds telling everybody to cut it out. Games of tag were crisscrossing each other so that one kid from one game would tag another kid from another game and then the two games would merge. The one painted hopscotch in the corner of the lot closest to the building became less like a game, in a place, and more like a through-station half the population was going to pass on their way to further fun someplace else. Hop one, two, three-four, five, six-seven, and away, never turning to hop back to one.

It would be tough enough under these conditions to get any kind of ballplaying done in the crowd, but there was no way we were not going to try, and no way anyone would try and stop us.

"You did pretty well with the snowballs," I said to Napoleon, "but have a look at this." As I said it, I drew a pimple ball out of the pocket of my jacket. It was the next best thing, the pimple ball, even though it bore very little resemblance to a baseball. It was small, and though it was white it was filled with air and covered with little bumps that had the added benefit of making it do strange little unpredictable fishtaily things when you put enough English on it. Life with the pimple ball was an important step on the baseball ladder, since we spent so many of our important hours in school, and real baseball was never going to happen on school grounds. It was also critical, skillwise, in that with a stick that was a lot skinnier than a bat, you were required to zero in on a ball much daintier than a hardball.

And about one tenth the size of the fat iceballs we had been murdering over the weekend.

He took the ball, squeezed it, tossed it up in the air a couple of times, then pointed.

He did that very well, I had to say. Silent and grim when he did it, Napoleon Charlie Ellis pointed me into the corner, farthest from the school building, where a weird small nook of the massive red church came together to form our natural St. C's home plate area. He had never yet played here but he knew. Another good indicator of NCE's instincts.

And when he did that, he looked like the Grim Reaper, ready to mow me down. No, more than that. He looked like Vida Blue of the Oakland A's. Now *that* was grim.

I stood in, and waited, scuffing the feet, gripping the bat, leaning.

And leaning, and leaning.

"What are you doing?" I asked as he backed farther and farther away from me, so far away that some of the space between us was being filled by a game of keepaway with Arthur Brown's shoe.

"Just stay in position," Napoleon said to me. I did, and then he finally stopped backtracking, leered in at me . . .

And started running my way.

I was stumped. I straightened up, started shouting at him to cut it out, but then instantly was shut up myself. After four or five long powerful strides, Napoleon's arm hanging behind his back, he left the ground and came over the top with a vicious whipping motion. I was then frozen, by the loud *whizzzz* of the pimple ball buzzing right past my face, ricocheting off both walls behind me, then rolling back out to Napoleon Charlie Vida Blue Ellis.

"Holy s-moke," was the best I could do.

That was the fastest anything had ever passed me without a driver inside it.

"What in the world was *that*?" I said, trying not to sound overly impressed.

"Bowling," he said, squeezing the ball, as if he was checking to see if he'd hurt it.

"Ah, excuse me, but I've been bowling lots, and it's much slower than that."

"Cricket. That's called bowling. Although if I had been properly bowling I would have bounced the ball off the ground before it reached you. I was trying to give you a chance."

"Try—" I could not even manage to finish the thought. I put that stick right back on my shoulder and planted. "Bowl," I said, nearly speechless at the thought of somebody having to give me a chance.

He took the ball, backed up, backed up, and came at me, hard.

In the ball came, spinning and wobbling and—

Whiffing. I lost my balance in the gritty wet pavement as I swung with everything to get that ball.

"Bowl," I yelled, as the ball reached Napoleon Charlie Ellis again.

"It does take some getting used to," he said kindly. "But you will learn to love it, I am sure of it."

"Bowl," I growled.

Bowl, he did.

Whiff. I was now losing my composure very quickly.

"I think maybe you need just to relax," he said.

A crowd began to gather around him. Tag games stopped. Arthur Brown got his shoe back. And Napoleon Charlie Ellis got his audience, just like when the photographers all surround the first pitchers to start their throwing down in Winter Haven.

I was hot. Yes the sun was out, and yes I was straining, but that was no excuse. I was hot, as in a sweaty brow, and damp armpits and there is no excuse for that kind of thing on a beautiful baseball day in February. I could sweat in a fancy restaurant because I didn't belong there. This was unacceptable. I *belonged* in this situation.

I became suddenly aware of being at the center of something, something that should have been great, that had always been great before. The sun was doing its job so well, melting the snow wherever it could, after Mr. Mendelson had done his job, plowing the whole yard down to nothing but watery icebanks along walls and fences. The whole place had a feel now like the base of a mountain when the winter was letting go and everything was wet with the snow being converted to crystal waters running down from the slopes. The ground everywhere was shiny.

And then I was unaware of it all again.

"Bowl," I said, and heard the odd little word repeated here and there in the crowd.

He looked at me without emotion. He nodded.

He stepped back and back and back, then forward, faster, faster, long went the stride, *sling*, over the top came the arm.

And *zzzzzip*, past me came the ball. I swung. But I was swinging at sound. I couldn't even see the pitch.

Napoleon bowled again, like I told him to. And bowled me out.

There was a lot of muttering out in the crowd, no laughing really, and no cheering. Because this was not the way things worked. I was supposed to be hitting these balls, for the whole school population probably as much as for myself. It was like the pond freezing solid in January, and the crocuses poking through the crust in March. I was supposed to be tattooing some poor pimple ball right now.

"Bowl," I said. Napoleon Charlie Ellis was trying to hold his game face, to show nothing, but the crack of a wince was coming across his tight lean skin.

"Maybe we should take a break, Richard," he said.

"Ya, Richard, take a break before you hurt yourself," Manny said, and a few people laughed.

I could feel the redness in my face, and was sure it could be seen from the cheapest seats in the house.

"Why are you lettin' him cheat?" Jum McDonaugh asked.

Napoleon turned to face him. "I do not cheat at anything," he said.

"You ain't supposed to run like that before pitching."

"It's okay," I said, frozen and probably looking crazy in my tight stance.

"Look," Jum said, walking up and taking the ball from Napoleon. He set himself, wound up, and slung one at me.

I have to confess, when I hit that pitch, when I hit the absolute guts out of that pitch, I almost cried with relief and excitement. I saw myself circling the bases, heard the theme to *Hawaii Five-O* blasting over the massive Fenway sound system, and felt like somebody had just pulled me up out of a pit of alligators.

"See," Jum said, as if he had accomplished some outstanding sports feat rather than giving up the biggest tater of the young season. "That is how to pitch a baseball."

"We were not playing baseball," Napoleon said. He took the ball again, as Arthur Brown ran it back from the far outfield. "We were playing cricket."

That's right, I thought. That's right, we weren't playing baseball. We were playing cricket. Oh, yes. God, yes. I was not failing at baseball, I was messing around with stupid old cricket. Yes. Yes. It was just cricket.

And the last time I would be playing cricket.

Jum screwed his face all up. *"Why?"* he asked.

"Because," Napoleon said, "Richard and I are thinking men, and so we play the thinking man's game."

Butchie stepped in and snatched the ball away from Napoleon. "Ya, well nobody plays that here."

"Some guys play it over at Franklin Park, every Sunday," Glen Solar said.

Butchie pointed at the ground under him. "But nobody plays it *here*," he said. "We play baseball here. Or stickball, but using baseball rules. Meaning, you don't run at the guy when you pitch to him. Cricket," he announced like some kind of authority, "is a stupid game."

"Cricket is not a stupid game," Napoleon said. "In fact, I believe that your inability to understand cricket is even further proof of the fineness of the game."

There were small titters of laughter that faded out as Butchie scanned the crowd. Then he trained his look back on Napoleon, who wasn't going anywhere.

I took a few steps toward them, caught Butchie's eye.

He upnodded at me. "Ya?" Then he ripped the stickbat out of my hand, and stared back at Napoleon.

"We got something to settle, Jiminy Cricket?" He waved the stick just slightly in Napoleon's direction.

"He probably can't even play baseball," Jum yelled, "that's why he has to play his retard game."

Butch laughed and nodded. I waited for Napoleon to say something, but instead a look of disgust came over his face and he started looking around, like he couldn't remember how he got into this.

Napoleon didn't much care what they thought. Whether he could play baseball or not. He was above that.

I wasn't.

"I pick Napoleon," I said.

Butch paused, grinned. "I'll take Jum."

"Manny."

"Glen."

"Quin."

"Arthur."

"My ball. We're up first."

The music was so loud in my head now, I could barely hear my teammates speaking to me.

"You'll do fine," I said to Napoleon. "You're a natural, remember? And you've been learning from the best."

I didn't notice, and didn't honestly care very much, what my other teammates had on their minds. The sun was out, I had the fever, I wanted to hit. I wanted us both to hit. Gold Dust moment.

And hit I did. Butchie was leering at me as I leaned in; he leaned back and let it fly. I don't think anyone was even surprised when I sent the thing back so swiftly and so hard that it caromed back off the highest bit of the school's four-floor face and came right back over Butchie's head and landed near home plate. I was already making my unnecessary trip around the bases—slap the fence pole for first, step on the joint between the two big pavement cracks for second, the rusty sewer grate for third—waving to the crowd and working on my spring tan. Good. Life. Good.

I did my bit. Normally after my bit I relax, calm down, lose interest. But my stomach now remained fluttery, my reflexes keen. There was more. I was waiting for it. Everybody was waiting for it.

Manny followed, getting cute by letting one slightly less than perfect pitch after another go past. He was antagonizing Butch, which was not only his right and normally satisfying, it was effective because Butch is easy to disturb. But I had no patience for it. This was not about Manny, and everyone was aware of that. "*Hit*," I screamed at him. The next pitch he delivered with a nice liner double, which was his usual. Quin followed by striking out on three pitches, which was his usual.

By the time Napoleon stepped up, with Manny on second, me catching, and Quin in a tag game somewhere,

I could see Sister Jacqueline coming out with the gong again. Rats. That meant that Butchie's team wouldn't get to hit, which was cool. But it also meant I might not get to bat again, which was very much not. More importantly, Napoleon wouldn't get to show his stuff.

"C'mon, c'mon, c'mon," I said, hurrying everyone.

Napoleon was holding his bat very low, so that he'd almost have to lift it up off the ground to hit the ball. I told him to pick it up, but then it was back down again. Some defensive cricket thing I was still to train out of him, but this was not the time. There was no time.

Butchie leaned back twice as far as normal and let it go.

Napoleon had been so crouched up on the plate, and so kind of sheepish about the whole thing, he almost didn't manage to fall out of the way in time.

The ball, buzzing at a serious speed, headed in on Napoleon, in farther, screwballing toward his head until it went even farther in, and behind him. Napoleon had to drop himself—and the bat in the bargain—to the ground in a jumble. The bat bounced, clattering tip to tip to tip, making a hollowed wood racket that echoed around the yard.

Napoleon got up slowly. He refused to give Butch the satisfaction of a look.

"Don't worry," I said when he looked to me. "That's just a brushback. It's his strategy. Look for the good one. He'll straighten it out."

Butchie smiled at the suggestion he might throw

something hittable. He leaned back again. I took my eye off him for half a second when the sun flashed off the bell that Sister J. was just now raising. It was so unfair.

Plunk. The second I turned back was the very second the pimple ball, coming awfully hard, was smacking Napoleon Charlie Ellis dead in the eye. It made a loud sharp sound, like if you slapped a raw chicken hard with your bare hand.

I jumped up. The bell was ringing *clang-a-lang-a-lang*, and the crowd was moving away.

"Jeez, sorry, man," Butchie said, as he strolled toward the line to go back inside.

I looked at Napoleon's eye. He tried to open it but it wanted to close, and did. Then he tried again, kept it open long enough for me to see it, pink with bloodshot, watery. And angry.

"He did that on purpose," Napoleon said.

I didn't answer. With most people I wouldn't need to.

"He hit me on purpose, Richard," Napoleon said, louder, covering his eye with his hand.

I found myself looking around, worried who might be listening. I couldn't believe it but he sounded like he was whining. You don't do that. You don't *do* that.

"No, he didn't hit you on purpose. He *threw* at you on purpose though. That's his job. *Your* job, Napoleon, is to get out of the way, and then be ready when a good pitch comes along. Then you show him who's boss. But you didn't do that."

It had to be clear. From the sound of my voice, it had to be clear. From Napoleon's reaction, I gathered that it was.

He forced the eye to stay open as he glared at me. The bell clanged again for us. "So it was my fault, is that what you are saying?"

"Oh, come on. Really, Napoleon, he's brushed me back a hundred times before."

"I am not *you*, am I?" he said, and as he said it he poked me hard in the chest with his finger, as if he was angry with *me*.

We walked to catch up with the rest of the line as they were filing in.

"Who cares who you are, all right? Pitchers throw at hitters. They don't just throw at *you*. Maybe if you'd stop worrying about who's doing what to *you* then maybe you'd be able to concentrate on playing, and not embarrass us both."

That was not how I meant to put it. I do better when I don't have a speaking part.

"I see," Napoleon said. He shook his head, then quick-stepped to leave me behind.

"I only meant it's just a regular part of the game," I called. He didn't answer.

I looked up at the blue blue sky. It had been such a perfect day before.

THERE
BUT
NOT
THERE

Over the next few days, winter returned, school fell into an even deeper than usual winter funk, and nobody seemed to really be talking to each other more than they needed to. It may have been just my impression, my feeling that because I wasn't right nobody was, but I don't think so. Because it is clear enough that when you get hit with a weirdly glorious early spring day everybody is talking more and running more and just stupidly happy more than they are normally stupidly happy. So why shouldn't it be that when that spring gift gets snatched away again, that good feeling goes right on out with it.

Anyway, I felt it. Maybe it was more, though. I suppose it could have been more.

Napoleon and I were okay, but not all the way. We saw each other a little less, which was fine since everybody needs to do that, to get out of each other's way some of the time. And he saw more of Beverly. Which was fine. It was fine.

Friday morning was the next time anybody tried to get a schoolyard game of stickball going. That somebody wasn't me, though. I squatted there on the sidelines, on my haunches, against the saggy ten-foot-high chain-link fence that separated St. Colmcille's from the mainstream of Boston. Sort of like the Vatican was separated from Rome, Sister Jacqueline once told us, there but not there at the same time. The cold had refrozen a lot of the drippy runoff of the snow, but conditions were not all that bad for a game, considering.

Still I squatted, thinking about getting in, thinking about not. Until Napoleon came along. He never rushed himself through lunch, regardless of the weather or the outside activities. Lunch is finished when it is finished, he'd say.

He came right over and squatted next to me, watching along with me as the other guys carried on without us. A ballgame with both of the Gold Dust Twins sitting out. Didn't make sense to me, but didn't seem to trouble anybody else much.

"I don't think we ever finished that discussion," Napoleon said out of practically nowhere.

"What discussion?"

"From the last time we were out here playing ball."

"Oh," I said, recalling what I had been trying hard not to recall. "I know. I don't want to talk about it, if it's all the same to you. I don't like talking about that stuff. I never have."

"So you admit, anyway, that there is a problem there."

"You think I could miss it? I just . . . would rather leave it alone, okay?"

Napoleon got very quickly and very seriously angry with me then. It took me by surprise.

"No. Richard. No, I don't believe it is all right to ignore it and pretend if we leave it alone it will go away. It won't, you know. It will only get worse, and you will have yourself very much to blame."

I felt like one of those prisoners in an old detective movie, being grilled and grilled in a dark dirty sweaty room until he snaps.

"Fine," I snapped. "I can't *stand* to be struck out. By anybody. Not even you. I hate it, and you struck me out about a million times, in front of a million spectators. But I'll get over it."

He was struck dumb. He slowly straightened up, stretched, and stood over me. "You know I'm not talking about that, don't you? You know I'm talking about what happened later."

I took a long breath. "Well, I don't *know* that, exactly . . . but I suppose I knew it was a possibility."

"Why do you have to do that?" he asked, taking his seat beside me again. At least we had made that much progress. "Richard, what good does it do you to avoid the bad things?"

"What good does it do *you* to go looking for them all the time?"

We sat, shut up, watched the game going on without us. We weren't done, though.

"So you believe that is all it was, just a regular part of the game."

"I believe that is what it is, a regular part of the game."

"Tell me then. When you do it, and someone gets hit, do you enjoy that part of it?"

"'Course not."

"Now. Did Butch enjoy hitting me?"

Why? Why did he have to do this?

"Napoleon," I said, shaking my head at the ground. I heard a lot of whooping and taunting that meant somebody had just knocked the ball out of sight. I wasn't interested. Shame, that.

"Napoleon, why do you want to go thinking about what's in somebody else's head? I think that's dangerous, you know, and it doesn't really get you anyplace. Not anyplace good, that's for sure."

He sighed, stood up again. I was hoping he wasn't going to put on the pressure for me to answer that question. I really didn't want to think about that question.

"You're right," he said, "we don't need to answer that question." And he walked away.

I don't think we were actually saying the same thing.

Friday evening, though, it was me and Napoleon, as planned, busing it out to the Westbrook Theater. We had this scheduled for over a week, as soon as I saw the Westbrook was bringing in *Bang the Drum Slowly*. It was an old-style big theater, with velvet seats and roof leaks so a lot of the time big sections of seats were roped off due to inclement weather. Most people were heading a couple miles up the parkway to the Showcase since they had four films going at once, and always had the newest releases, but I always preferred the Westbrook even if they brought in movies like *Bang the Drum Slowly* only after they had been around the block—okay, the world— a couple dozen times already. The concession stand was not exactly separated from the auditorium so much as it was just around a bend from it. That was good, because you could smell the popcorn very well and could still listen to the dialogue when you went to get some.

And *Bang the Drum Slowly*, with Robert DeNiro, playing in the Westbrook and no place else, was a baseball movie. That was all I needed to know about it.

"That is a very funny theater," Napoleon said as we exited the wide, well-lit lobby.

"Ya," I said, offering him a sip of my Coke, "I knew you would love it."

He took the Coke. Sipped silently, even though it was very near the bottom of the cup and the ice should have been making a big noise. "I did not say I loved it."

I took the Coke back. "Ya, but I can tell. Want some Junior Mints?"

He took some Junior Mints. Offered me some Good & Plenty. I took one, to be sociable, but Good & Plenty are awful, and I thought everybody knew that. In fact I believed that the boxes in the display case were dummies, empty cartons left there for the old-timey look.

"How can you tell, Richard? What I love and what I do not love?"

As agreed, we were walking along the small piece of sidewalk that connected all the mini-mall stores, past Bea's Dress Shop and Hallmark Cards, over to Friendly's for an ice cream.

"I don't know, I just can, that's all. Some stuff I just figure a guy's gotta love. Just makes sense."

"Mmm," he said. He pushed the door to Friendly's open, and let me in first. "So, did I love the film?"

"Oh ya," I said. "Of course." I pointed toward the back, to a booth, and he shook his head. We sat at counter stools.

"Well, I did not," he said. "It was all right, but I thought it was a bit boring at times."

"Boring? Boring? Are you—" Suddenly it occurred to me that, of course he was. "Ah, you're just trying to get me going."

"Get you going where? I did not like the film very much."

"What are you *talking* about? There was baseball all over the place." I was raising my voice just a little bit, and waving my arms around, as if to show Napoleon Charlie Ellis the baseball all over the place.

The waitress came over. "Can you please stop shouting?" she said to Napoleon.

"Excuse me?" Napoleon snapped.

"He wasn't shouting, it was me," I said. "And I wasn't shouting."

"Yes, you were shouting," Napoleon said, staring deep into his menu as if he was embarrassed to be seen with me. And, of course, angry. "And *I* naturally get the blame for it."

"Banana Boat," I whispered to the waitress. She nodded.

Napoleon curled his lip. "I will have a bowl of strawberry. With strawberry sauce, please."

We sat for a couple of minutes then, as the waitress went about her work. We stared at her, then at the flavor roster high above the counter. Then we stared at her some more. Then finally stared at each other, in the yellowy mirror across from us.

"It was a great movie," I said.

"It was not," he said, "but there were some fine things in it."

"Like the baseball," I said.

I was trying Napoleon's patience. Maybe not completely by accident. "The baseball in that film," he said firmly, "did not look very good to me. I think you are a better baseball player than anyone we saw tonight."

I had only been half-listening to what Napoleon was saying, because I was so stirred up at the fact that he was saying it at all. I pointed a finger at his reflection and opened my mouth to snap, when the words finally caught up with my brain.

"Oh," I said. "Well. I guess . . . y'know, for such a disagreeable guy, you sure do know how to disagree in a good way."

He laughed. Our ice creams arrived. We attempted to be quiet again for a minute while we ate. Napoleon was pretty fair at being quiet for spells. That made one of us.

"So what was good in there, do you think?" I asked through a mouthful of banana and marshmallow.

He held up a finger while he quickly swallowed a spoonful of strawberry. I don't think he was expecting to have to speak again that soon. And if you get one of those big hard frozen berries in there . . .

"Oh . . . oh . . ." Napoleon said, raising his hands to his temples and squinting hard.

"Take a half-spoonful and hold it on the roof of your mouth for five seconds," I said, giving him the rescue dose out of my dish.

He did, and I could see relief come to his face. Success.

"Good work," he said. "Thank you."

"I'm surprised you didn't know that one, man. I've frozen my head a thousand times and it always works. Jeez, there is still so much you haven't learned."

He turned to the real me, not the mirror me. "I have a history of taking reasonable bites, and of swallowing my food completely before speaking."

"Ah," I said, mouth once more full, "I'll help you get over that too."

I guess that was funny, because Napoleon laughed. And he continued looking at me. It was a strange picture now, with me eating, Napoleon staring at the side of my head, while I looked at him looking at me in the mirror. It was a picture I had not had before, watching him watching me. I did not know Napoleon Charlie Ellis as an overly smiley guy, as an easygoing guy, or even, you could say, as a warm guy. But there he was, once removed, almost as if he couldn't tell I was watching. And so he was different. I could see him, guard down, enjoying himself. Smiling at Richard Riley Moncrief. Being easy with him. Liking him.

I turned quickly to face the real Napoleon, not the mirror one. Just as quickly he turned back toward his dish. Easier that way. For us both.

"Friends," he said.

I stopped eating, but looked again at him in the mirror.

"In that movie. The friends, that pitcher and catcher. They were great and unusual friends. That was something fine to watch for one and a half hours. That was indeed very fine."

Somewhere in there, I liked this. Though it was just a movie, after all. And at the same time it made me a little bit squirmy. Though it was just a movie, after all.

"Um-hmm," I said. "Too bad he had to die. And that he was a half-wit."

"Yes. And there was one thing, one big thing, that I think they got quite wrong. When that catcher asks if everyone has begun being kind to him simply because they know he is dying."

"Right," I said, taking a wild swing. "Like it would really matter."

"No," Napoleon answered. "I believe it matters very much. But I don't think the pitcher's answer was an honest one. He said, 'Everybody knows everybody's dying, and that's why people are as good as they are.'"

I dropped my spoon into my empty bowl. "Ya, I remember that now. I thought that was really great. I loved that part. What was wrong with that?"

Sometimes, I could get the quick shock of a feeling that what I said could make Napoleon Charlie Ellis very sad and disappointed, and I did not know why or how to stop doing it. This was one of those times.

"I have moved three times in my life already, Richard Riley Moncreif, and the more new people I meet the less anyone seems to know about anyone else. And when you meet someone who is different, *den dat* is a remarkable *ting*."

It was the first time. The first time I had heard it all peeled away, and heard Napoleon sound anything like his father. And he was breathing heavily, directly into my ear, as if this was an effort for him, and at the same time some kind of challenge, a dare, to me.

One that I did not understand.

"I'm sorry. That you had to move so much," I said. "Maybe if you stayed in the same place you'd get to know people better. And they would *be* better. Maybe this is your stop. Maybe it'll happen here."

"Boston?" he said, raising one eyebrow high. "That's not what the papers say."

"Well, first thing is, stop looking at the papers."

"All right. So when are we getting together then, you and I and our fathers?"

Sigh. I was so pleased to see Napoleon sort of warming up. But at the same time . . .

It wouldn't do either of us any good to be pretending.

"Okay, second thing is, maybe you should stop asking for that. It wouldn't . . . be a good mix."

He nodded, like he had an equation just now worked out. Only he didn't look satisfied or relieved, like a regular guy would.

"Richard, are you saying that reading about Boston or meeting your people won't be helpful in straightening me out? Is that what you're saying?"

I was approaching overload. *No*, Napoleon, just *cut it out* . . . all the time with this stuff. Always, always, he had to make it harder when it didn't have to be.

I started humming. To the movie tune. *So bang the drum slowly . . . and play the fife lowly*

"Richard?"

"No. What I'm saying is, can't you just know a guy for the guy, and not think about where he comes from or who he lives with or whatever?"

He let the words float in the air. So we could both hear them. I think we both did.

"Good question," he said.

He may have been waiting for me to give the answer. If I knew what it was I would have given it. But he wasn't solving it either, so I was more than ready to move on to questions we could deal with.

"You gonna finish that?" I asked, pointing to his melting strawberry with puddled strawberry sauce.

He slid me the plate, shaking his head.

GONE
BANANAS

"So where's your sister?" Butchie wanted to know.

I looked at Beverly, and she looked at me. We were sitting side by side in gray metal folding chairs in the school's ancient auditorium, St. Gerald's Hall. We were supposed to be listening to instructions on how we were going to wow the locals as a school-sized choir this upcoming Palm Sunday. Beverly and I were in the mime section of the choir. We didn't need to listen all that closely. Butchie was the one member of the class so incredibly unaware of being unmusical he was *asked* not to sing, so he too had time on his hands.

"Who are you asking?" I asked.

"Both of you."

"What sister would that be, Butch?" Beverly said wearily.

"Sister Mowgli," he laughed.

"Would you just cut that stuff out, Butch?" she snapped. "Don't be a goon *all* the time."

"Ya, give the guy a break," I said.

He ignored me. "So Bevvy, are you goin' with that guy now or something?" Butch asked.

The room was suddenly filled with two hundred voices, singing in lots of different keys.

"What's it to you?" she asked.

"Ya, turn around, and don't sing, Butch," I said.

"Too bad Mowgli's not here. We'd sound a lot better. We could do all that calypso and stuff. Maybe they'll let us do 'Yellow Bird' for Palm Sunday, you know, with palm trees and stuff."

I picked both feet up off the floor and gave Butch's chair a shove. This sent him just far enough forward to bang him into some eighth grade girl, who happened to be one of the real singers, not to mention a world-class moaner, the way eighth grade girls seem to be. The girl let out a good loud one, bringing the raggedy version of "I Just Had to Pray" to a painful halt. Which naturally brought Sister Jacqueline and her long waggy finger to Butchie.

The organ music rose, like the backing track to some old horror movie, and as he was hauled away and Beverly and I shook hands, Butch threw me a glare. "Thanks, *Riley*," he mouthed, using the name he prefers I'd use. Fair enough, I might say under the circumstances, except it was a lot harder and more mean than what I'd seen out of him before. He'd done as much to me lots of times, and I figured to be able to get away with more than this with him.

"Hah," Beverly said as the music whined once more. "Serves him right, the animal."

"Ya," I agreed. "I mean, it's none of his business, and you're not going with Napoleon anyway."

There in the middle of all that sound of music, was a big fat silence.

"Right?" I added, awkwardly.

She was staring at me now. "What difference does it make?"

Fair enough question. There was something, a feeling, swirling around in my belly, though. Wasn't good. Wasn't familiar. Whatever it was, I probably had no business feeling it.

"Nothing," I said. "No difference. Forget about it."

Beverly wasn't the forget-about-it kind. Something else she had in common with Napoleon.

"What, Richard, it's one thing when you spend time with him but when I do it there's something wrong? What's he, not my *type*? Is that it? That better not be it, Richard. I hope it's just something stupid like you're jealous of him . . . or of me. . . ."

It felt like it didn't even matter what was right anymore. With every word my head sank lower like a whipped dog's. "I'm sure it's something stupid, Beverly. I guarantee it's just something stupid."

"Mmm," she said. "Well, smarten up, Richard. Quickly."

What else could I say? "Okay. I'm smartening up." I even believed that was true. I wasn't unteachable after all.

We left it there. We both tried to join the singing for

real, which was a mistake. People started looking at us. We went back to miming.

"I wonder where he is anyway," Beverly said. "This is two days in a row. I hope he's all right."

"I think he's fine," I answered. "He was on the field with me every afternoon for the whole week, before this."

She turned, and lightly bopped me off the side of the head. "You psycho. Have you been dragging that poor guy out in this miserable weather every day to play baseball?"

"It has not been mis—"

"Not for *you*, it hasn't. 'Cause you're a mutant baseball-demented polar bear, *Riley*. Napoleon is from a tropical climate. He's only been here for a few months. You could kill him, forcing him to be like you." She bopped me again.

"I didn't force him," I said. "He loves to play. Why else would he?"

"Because he has basically no friends, other than us."

"Oh, that isn't even true," I said, with no evidence to back me up. In fact, I knew what she said was true. But he had me, I figured, and we had fun.

"You need to start wearing your batting helmet more, Richard. You're a little out of it, and I think you're getting worse."

"No, really, if Napoleon has no friends it's because he doesn't want any. Why else would it be?"

"Well, this isn't really a very friendly place, is it? You might even say it can be hostile. Or mean."

"Don't you think that's a little strong, Beverly? It's got

its problems, but . . . I mean, I've been in this school for—"

As nuns can do, Sister Jacqueline appeared like a puff of smoke, leaning right down in front of my face. "You will be next, Mr. Moncreif, unless you stop chatting, and start mouthing the words to this hymn."

Even she knew about the miming.

It was all business from that point, but there was no shortage of facemaking between Beverly and me. She kept going back to one in particular, where she would wrinkle her brow, *tsk-tsk* me, and screw down one side of her mouth, to point out how clueless I supposedly was.

"I don't think it's as bad as that," I whispered when the coast was clear enough. I made an effort to keep mouthing the approximate words everyone else was singing, while still getting out the words I was thinking. I must have looked like one of those dubbed Godzilla movies.

"Of course you don't," Beverly answered, doing the same thing. And yes, she did look like the Godzilla movies. "You think it's wonderful here because it is wonderful for *you* here, because you have been here forever. You think everything will be great as long as you keep teaching Napoleon baseball in the daytime and taking him to boring baseball movies at night."

"Hey," I snapped, stretching it out to look like I was snapping "Hallelujah," "I think it's a good thing to show him our *national pastime*, instead of dragging him to see *The Great Waldo Pepper* like you would probably do."

"You know, I would love to take him to *The Great Waldo Pepper*. But guess what I would do first? I would *ask* the guy what *he* wanted to see."

She had done it now. I didn't quite know how she had done it, but she had.

"He *loved* the movie," I said loudly, blowing my cover completely. "He loved *Bang the Drum Slowly*."

I did not notice the music dying down, but I did notice the voice speaking to me.

"Mr. Moncreif," Sister Jacqueline said, "lend me your ear." And before I had the chance to lend it to her or not, she took it, hard.

As we sat there in the office, no sound happening other than the organ and voices off in the distance, the feeling between Butchie and me was weird. We just stared for the longest time.

"Tsamatter with you lately?" I asked finally.

"Tsamatter with *you* lately?"

"What are you talking about, Butch?"

"You too good to hang out with us anymore? Where you been? What you doing?"

"I been around. I been doing stuff."

"Not with me you ain't."

"Oh. Oh, I get it. You mean baseball."

"Well, duh. You don't *do* nothin' else."

"Oh I do loads else, don't give me that. Anyway, I've been playing almost every day, so I don't know what you're moaning about."

"Ain't been playing with me. Ain't been playing with Quin or nobody else I know of. We ain't been playing any ball."

"Napoleon's been throwing to me," I said. "He's not afraid of the weather like the rest of you guys. You know you can come on down anytime you want to. You know where we are."

"Nnn," he said, shaking his head. "Your friend wouldn't like that. He's too good for us. Don't want to dirty his hands with neighborhood trash like us."

"That's just stupid, Butchie, and you—"

"He don't mind handling our girls, though, huh?"

I practically spat on him, laughing. "Our girls? I didn't even realize we *had* any girls. Jeez, you think I'd notice a thing like that."

Butchie's always-shaky sense of humor was all the way gone these days. He got up, walked across the bit of carpet between us, and stood over me. I stayed in my seat, staring up.

"You know what I'm talking about, Riley. Guy like that, comes in here out of noplace—"

"Dominica. Not noplace, Dominica. It is a place. An island, actually."

"Comes in here, to our place, starts looking down his nose at scumbags like me, brings in his smartass father to show off even more, then goes after the . . . local girls, like he's just picking one more banana off his own personal tree."

I stood up. I still had to look up at him. "What's this

thing you got with bananas lately?"

I wanted him to laugh, to see how stupid this all was. And I wanted him to shut up. People don't have to be perfect for life to go on okay, they just have to be good enough. They just have to not be awful.

And even while I was saying it to myself, I knew it was already too late. And I knew he couldn't keep it to himself just because I wanted it that way.

"I *hate* bananas," he said, real nasty, real close. His breath stank, like bacon gone raunchy.

"Are the two of you going to be a full-time job for me today?" Sister said as she stepped in between us. "I don't know what has gotten into you, but get it the hell out, right now." She used the word "hell" regularly and freely, and in many different ways, which I admired.

"Yes, Sister," we both answered.

"Now the two of you get back to the class, and tell them I will be along in five minutes so get busy in the meantime."

"Yes, Sister." We sounded like zombies.

We walked back to class, near each other, but not really together. We didn't talk until we were about to go through the door. I put a hand on his shoulder as he peeked through the window and made a face at everybody. He stopped, turned, and stared at the hand before looking at my face.

"You know, Butch, you've only been here since halfway through last year yourself, so as far as I'm concerned you're about as foreign as Napoleon."

I thought I was reasoning with him.

He took a deep loud breath through his nose, then removed my hand from him like it was a snotted-up Kleenex.

"How stupid are you, Riley?" he asked and then walked through the door.

I was getting pretty sick of that question.

IMPOSSIBLE
DREAM

When I called him on the phone I was again surprised at how islandy Napoleon could sound if all you had to focus on was his voice. He sounded older too. And right now, a lot slower.

"Hey," I said. I wasn't a natural with the phone.

"Richard? Is that you?"

"Ya. How's it going?"

"Well. I haven't been well. Not well a'tall. Getting better, though."

It never took me long to run low on conversation on the telephone. "Hey. You're good on the phone, huh? Like a different guy. Like a pro."

"Thank you, I suppose."

"So," I said. "Just kind of wondered, y'know, where you were, how you were, that kind of thing. Been missing some pretty funny choir practices, you know."

Napoleon sighed. He was sounding sadder than I had

figured, what with the vacation from school and all.

"I am sorry to be missing them," he said. "I will not be missing the performance, though."

"You sound like you *want* to do it. But that couldn't be true."

"I do. Very much so. I love music."

Huh? This was news. This was *such* news, and while being weird and interesting, it felt to me suddenly sad. If, like Beverly said, he didn't have any other friends, then shouldn't I have been the guy knowing things like this? Even if I didn't much want to know about his music, I would still want him to tell me about it.

"You do? Really? How come I never knew that? What kind of music? Not church music."

"Yes. I love church music. Also James Brown, and the Ohio Players. Bob Marley and Jimmy Cliff. Organ music of all kinds, I love."

Way out of my league now. But I had to try. "Ever hear John Kiley? He's the guy who plays that really loud organ at Fenway. And did you know he's the same guy who plays for the Bruins and Celtics at the Garden? Now that's talent, huh?"

He waited. I thought I had carried that off pretty well, but in the break it occurred to me that he could be laughing with his hand over the phone. Or gagging or something.

"I will go hear him sometime," Napoleon said politely. I was grateful for those manners of his. But still, this did not feel quite right.

"Can I say something?" I asked.

"That is about all one can do on the telephone."

"Well, you don't sound good. I mean, you don't sound sick, but you don't sound so . . . good."

Pause. Longer pause. "I am. I am . . . good. Thank you."

"You're . . . welcome. Did I do something wrong, Napoleon?"

"No."

"You mad about something?"

"No."

"You want to tell me something?"

"No."

"Something happen to you that I should know about?"

"No, and no, and no. Don't you ever . . . Richard, don't you ever have those days when you're just feeling down? It is normal, no? They come and they go, don't they? Doesn't that happen to you?"

I actually had to give this some thought. Had to kind of search around in my insides for something loose in there. I did as thorough a search as I could.

"No," I said. "I have to be honest with you. No. Sure, I have a beef here and there like anybody. But you know, I don't mostly feel like I have a lot to gripe about." I shrugged, even though that wouldn't contribute much to the conversation. "My life's pretty okay, as far as I can tell."

This produced our longest pause yet. Felt like it was nearly as long as the talking part of talking.

Stupid, stupid, Richard. It was as if I was looking for the most unhelpful thing to say. "Of course *you* don't think things are so bad here," was what Beverly had told me. I had it all here, and I knew it. Napoleon did not, and I knew that too.

"Do you miss home, Napoleon?" I asked this as easily and quietly as I could, though I had no business doing it. One week at a camp two hours away was the greatest separation I had ever endured. It was at a lake, in July, with half of my friends. It was *better* than being home. I knew nothing about what he was living through, and had no right going into it.

I felt like I had to go into it.

I heard a rapid series of short shallow wispy breaths, like a muffled asthma attack. He would not talk. Then it went quieter, like he was covering the receiver with his hand. I waited, until I couldn't stand it anymore.

"It's probably just me," I said tentatively. "Maybe there's just something wrong with me. You know. No brain, no pain?"

Nothing.

"Ignorance is bliss, right?" I tried, brighter.

For this, he came back.

"Getting warmer," he mumbled.

Which, after all that, was what cut. I could feel the smile slither off the edges of my face. I thought I was on his side. I thought I was helping. I thought I was doing good. I had been trying to cheer him up a bit, and could feel the actual sting in the middle of it.

In the middle of me.

"Oh," I said, my voice sounding probably worse than Napoleon's. "I get it."

"Wait, Richard," he said.

I didn't.

I lay down on my bed, grabbed the ball off the night table, and began bouncing it off the ceiling and catching it. Bouncing it off the ceiling and catching it.

Why couldn't I seem to get through a single conversation anymore? Why did things have to be hard for no good reason? Did I owe somebody an apology for liking things pretty much the way they were?

Were happy and stupid both the same thing?

I could smell spring. All things right were about to come together, just like they did this time every year, so why shouldn't I feel okay? Why couldn't I?

My ball began making a foreign sound. For every bounce off the ceiling I was hearing a shadow bounce. Twinned. I don't know how long it was happening before it occurred to me to go to the window, but Napoleon Charlie Ellis looked pretty cold by the time I saw him throw that last leather ball, *thump*, off my storm window.

I opened the sash, opened the storm.

"What's that?" I asked coolly.

"Cricket ball."

"Looks stupid."

He wanted to say something back. Would have had

the right. He didn't, though. He threw the ball straight up in the air and caught it again.

"Coming down?" he asked.

"What are you doing out?"

"Feeling better." He was working on not showing any face. No smile, frown, scowl. The phone Napoleon was separated, different. Like the mirror Napoleon at the ice-cream parlor. Different characters from the poker-faced guy with the cricket ball. "Coming down?"

"What? To play cricket?"

"Maybe. If you like. Or baseball. No matter."

The impulse in me, the dumb impulse, was to grab the Adirondack and hit the stairs.

"Tomorrow," I said, without an explanation.

Napoleon Charlie Ellis nodded. Then he short-armed a throw that almost caught me off guard, but didn't. It came up on a line, face high, through the eight-inch opening of the storm window. I caught it at my ear.

"Have that," he said, backing away.

I looked at the hard reddish leathery ball. Squeezed it, rolled it around in my hand.

I looked back down at Napoleon. He wasn't one hundred percent different from me. He did better when he shut up too.

"Thanks," I said, and shut the window.

REAL
SPRING

It was a couple of weeks into March before real spring started setting in, and playing ball became more of a part of everybody's days. Partly because of the weather, and partly because of the daily reports coming up from Florida. It was becoming obvious to the world. Fred Lynn was special. The Gold Dust Twins were special. And the 1975 Red Sox were going to be something we would remember for the rest of our lives.

If I wasn't playing baseball I was watching it. And if I wasn't watching it in the real world I was watching it in my head. Napoleon and I had played so much repetitive two-man baseball, we were getting to know each other's game as well as we knew our own. He was beginning to learn how I would set him up with a couple of off-speed junky pitches, then try to sneak the third past him with a short-delivery fastball. We would go to the frozen field down off the parkway, or more often the defrosting, muddy field, with a duffel bag full of bruised, scarred, or waterlogged balls, and take turns emptying the bag on each other. I loved to hit still, and if I could there would be days when I never surrendered the bat to him, and I know that would have been fine with Napoleon too. Because he loved to throw.

He certainly loved to throw.

Napoleon Charlie Ellis could *throw* a baseball.

But I couldn't do that because that was not the plan. We could not be the Gold Dust Twins if we did not have well-rounded skills. People were already making fun of Jim Rice's fielding ability down there in Winter Haven, as if being able to hit a baseball from Florida to Georgia was not enough, and I was not going to let that happen to Napoleon.

Fred Lynn could do *everything*, though. It was awesome.

Besides, we did ourselves so much good with our constant hit-and-pitch routine. I could see it every time out, as Napoleon's stroke got smoother, stronger, more controlled. I didn't have to guide him as much anymore but there were still occasions when I would step down off the mound and sidle up next to him, showing him one small fine adjustment or another. Only there was this progression happening where with each attempt, I would find him a little stiffer, a little less pliable than before until, by the last time I tried to help him, he had changed from the Gumby poseable figure I started out with into a bronze statue. His stance was his stance, and as I tried to get the tiniest of changes out of him, we locked into this struggle of will and muscle, Napoleon holding stubbornly steady, me trying to bend his left arm slightly . . . Napoleon stiffening . . . me bending . . . until . . . the bat fell away completely, I grabbed his shirt, he gave me a headlock . . . and the two of us toppled into the sloppy soupy mush of the batter's box.

We wrestled there for a few seconds, not to establish who was going to beat the other, certainly not to settle the batting-stance question, but to make sure neither of us got back up with one single patch of unmudded clothes.

And the laughing made it even harder to get back up on our feet. We sat there for a few seconds.

"There," I said. "Much better."

I got up and headed back to the mound calmly.

"Next time," Napoleon called, "I'll come visit you out there and show *you* how to pitch."

"Hah. That'll be the day," I said.

But really, I knew he very well could. I could swear that every day his fastball gained one more mile per hour.

He was already the hardest thrower I had ever seen.

"I have to tell you something, Richard," he said as we went through our routine, combing the outfield together to gather up the balls for the next guy to pitch. We were playing till we dropped that day, and nobody was complaining but the balls. I had pitched a full bag already to Napoleon, and he had just finished doing the same for me. When we gathered up this bunch, we would start the whole thing over again. "I thought today was the day. I thought today you were not going to keep up."

I stopped right there in my tracks, ankle deep in grassy mud. "You thought *I* . . . ?" I pulled one of the balls back out of the bag, held it up between us like that guy with the skull in *Hamlet*. "You know what this *is*? You know who *I* am?"

"Yes, I know you both," he said dryly. "But I have been feeling so strong these last few days, as if the ball is simply going to go faster and faster every time. You know that feeling?"

Did I know it? I had often wondered if I would ever hear anyone else say what I thought so many times before. This was how I figured parents feel when their kids graduate or are born or get married or something. I nodded and went back to picking up balls.

"But every time, you catch up. You learn. You *make* yourself hit the ball when it appears that you are falling behind."

I looked at him again, and spoke as seriously as I could. "I *really* want to hit that ball."

"Yes. I can see that."

"Thanks. You make me better." I felt I couldn't come up with any higher praise than that. Or any greater thanks.

"You actually do intend to play baseball for all your life, don't you, Richard."

We had now collected all the balls and were walking back toward the infield. We almost never spoke anymore when we were hitting, so this was our moment. I grew to like this bit very much. It would have been my favorite part of the entire drill, if hitting and pitching weren't the other parts.

"Of course I'm going to play pro ball. The only people who don't want to are the people who can't. And you're coming with me. We're the Gold Dust Twins, remember. Only we'll have to think up a different name by then."

We were both standing on the mound. Napoleon had both feet on the rubber, as he would be if he was looking for the sign from the catcher. I was in front of him, on the home plate side, with the duffel bag slung over my shoulder. Because it was my turn to pitch.

He shook his head at me.

"What, no?" I asked. "Oh, listen, don't worry. You are good enough, I know this stuff. And hey, even if you were borderline, I'd do that thing like in *Bang the Drum Slowly* . . . you know, put in my contract, wherever I go, my buddy goes."

He continued to shake his head, but added the words. "Thank you very much, Richard. I'm glad you would do that for me. But that's not it. The difference is not that you can play and I cannot. The difference is that you *want* to."

I dropped the bag of balls at my feet. I swear I had never considered this, that Napoleon Charlie Ellis wouldn't want to play baseball for life. That *anybody* wouldn't. How could this be true? How could somebody with Napoleon's ability not want to spend his life playing ball? He had the *feeling*, I was sure I had heard it, just minutes before, when he was describing the feeling of getting better and better with every pitch, of getting better than yourself, of getting better than everybody else. I knew he was feeling it because he was describing what I had always felt like nobody else was ever able to describe. I knew it before that, even just by watching him play, by watching him improve faster than I could have imagined. Because he was made for this game.

He could not be right. If he was still a little short of full commitment to the *game* the *idea* the *life* of baseball, it wasn't because it wasn't in there. It was because I had just not finished the job of helping him along.

I couldn't imagine it any other way.

"You can't really be serious," I said, because if I tried to say it all, I would sound crazy.

He shrugged. "Yes, I can. I like playing here and now, though. I like that very much. And I am happy if I am helping you get better and closer to your dream. But that is it. The rest, that is *your* dream. It is not mine."

He didn't even look sorry.

"You're not joking, by any chance, Napoleon?"

He stomped down off the mound, right up to me, and gave me a good stiff shove in the chest before blowing by me on the way to the plate. "I hope to love something as insanely as you do baseball, Richard Riley Moncreif. Because if I do, whatever it is I will be the world's greatest at it." He picked up the Adirondack.

I picked up the glove and slipped it onto my hand. If I

coated my hand in raw pizza dough, it would not mold to me any closer than this glove that I had lived with, literally slept with, breaking it in under my mattress with a ball stuck in the web.

I picked up a ball, aimed it at Napoleon. "Ah, you'll change your mind. I know you will."

I threw him the straight hard one that he could hit a mile.

He hit it a mile.

I watched the ball every inch of the way, with my arms stretched wide, the scent of mud and grass in my nose, water in my shoes, and cool wind on my face.

No matter what he thought, Napoleon Charlie Ellis was a baseball player.

YARD
DOGS

Palm Sunday. I had no idea.

"Where'd you learn to do that?" I asked, and I was aware of sounding like a fan. But he was so shockingly good, there was nothing else I could do.

"I learned at church," Napoleon said. "Isn't that where most people learn?"

"No. I've been going to church every Sunday since I was six years old, sometimes even more than once a week depending on holy days and weddings and funerals and stuff. I have heard zillions of singers, heard enough organ music to fill probably a year's worth of time solid, and I have been instructed at least one period a week for all of my school life. And I still sound like this."

Without hesitation or modesty, I lit into a version of "Ave Maria," right there in the street within spitting distance of the church itself. I sang strong, and I sang loud because I did not know how to sing it any other way, and

I sang so bad that if there were any birds in the area they would have fallen dead out of the trees. Napoleon reached out and clapped both hands over my mouth, and while that would under normal circumstances be a pretty hostile move, I did not take offense. Because he did it out of respect for music, and he was right to do it. I am an insult to music and musicians everywhere.

"Wow," Napoleon Charlie Ellis said.

"Wow is right," I answered.

"Wow," Beverly said, running up and wedging herself in between us.

"What are you doing here?" I asked her. The Ward 17s never showed up at our church on Sundays. They had their own church, and while the Catholic schools were filling up all over the city, the actual churches weren't selling out most home games.

"I came for the show," she said. "Na*pol*eon," she added, with a slap on his arm, "why didn't you tell us you were some kind of musical genius?"

"Stop it," Napoleon said, pulling away from her. When we caught up to him, he reversed direction and started walking quickly back in the direction of church.

"And he's a *shy* superstar, at that," Beverly said.

"Hey," I said, catching up and clutching at his shirt so the brilliant white tail of it came flapping out of his pants. "I knew him first. I knew him when he was a regular guy."

"I hate it when this happens," Napoleon said. Now he

stopped running east or west. He simply stopped right there in the sidewalk, clenched his fists and shut his eyes, as if he was going to make us disappear.

"When this happens?" Beverly and I said together.

"What are you, Napoleon, some fugitive from fame? Does this happen to you a lot? Are you some kind of child prodigy, like Donny Osmond?"

"*Now* you are making me angry," Napoleon said, opening his eyes briefly, then snapping them closed again.

"Excuse me?" Someone was calling, and waving, from the front of the church. He was a tall thin man, with glasses and a very neat gray suit on. His shoes made a loud clicking sound as he hurried our way. He looked so anxious to get to us that it couldn't have been good.

"Did you do something wrong?" I asked Beverly as the man approached.

"No. I figured it was one of you guys."

Napoleon had his eyes wide open now and stood tall as the man approached. "I don't care what he wants. I am pleased just to change the subject."

"Young man," the man said, reaching for Napoleon's hand, "your singing was breathtaking." He must have been telling the truth, since he was breathless.

"Thank you," Napoleon said shyly.

"My name is James Connolly, and I'm from the Archdiocese Choir School. Have you heard of it?" He continued holding Napoleon's hand. He was no longer shaking it, just holding on and smiling like he was some sort of great lifelong admirer of Napoleon's work.

"No, sir, I've never heard of the Archdiocese Choir School, or any other choir school, as a matter of fact."

"Well, that's fine. Wouldn't want some other denomination recruiting you away from us," Mr. Connolly said, and chuckled musically. "Seriously. Have you had any serious training, Mister . . . ?"

"Ellis. And no, I have never actually trained."

"Ever thought about it? No, never mind. Don't answer that. I'll be around to all the classes on Monday. We can talk more about it then." He started shaking again, then backed away quickly, so as not to upset the great performer I guess.

With Mr. Connolly gone, I had no qualms about upsetting the great performer.

"Ar, ar, arrr," I laughed out loud. "Can you believe that guy? A school? For choir?"

"I think it sounds great," Beverly said. "You deserve it, Napoleon, you lucky thing. We're going to miss you, though."

"What?" I said loudly. We had absently turned and were once again floating down the sidewalk away from church. "What are you talking about, Beverly? You don't really think Napoleon would be interested in leaving to go to some weenie choir school?"

"Of course he would. He'd be crazy not to."

By now even I could see that Napoleon Charlie Ellis was not participating in the discussion of the future of

Napoleon Charlie Ellis. It seemed that there was now a lot going on in that head, with small flicks of different expressions snapping across his face and then leaving to be replaced by something else. Confusion was in the mix. Then fear. Excitement, then something else again.

"What's up, Napoleon?" I asked.

"You all right?" Beverly asked.

He looked straight ahead, then at me, then at Beverly, then straight ahead again. Now he looked like he had just woken up from a pleasant dream.

"I never heard of such a thing," he said. It wasn't so much a yea or a nay to the choir school idea, but an amazement over the plain fact of its existence.

"I hear you, man. The world's gone nuts. Come on, let's go play some baseball."

"Would you pa-lease," Beverly scolded me. "Just give it a rest for one day, huh? Anyway, I was thinking you guys might like to go for a little ride today. I know a great Brigham's in a great square, all old-timey, and clean. My treat."

"Ya?" I said. "Well, Whatcha think, choir-boy?"

Napoleon scowled at me. Then he looked to Beverly, sort of nervous and embarrassed at the same time. "Ah, well, you mean in your neighborhood? Would that be a good idea?"

"No," Beverly said boldly, "that would not be a good idea, I'm ashamed to say. But this is not in my neighborhood. It's in that direction, but not quite. Neutral territory."

It was amazing to me the way a small statement like that could change Napoleon's whole face. From closed up and scowling to smooth in seconds. From mean old man to twelve-year-old regular guy. "I would be pleased to go," he said to her.

By the time we got there it seemed like the day was nearly gone. Wait for the bus, ride the bus. Wait for the other bus, ride the bus. All the while I couldn't help staring and staring into the blue sky dotted with the occasional bit of a cloud, and all around sprayed with bright sunshine. Napoleon and Beverly were most of the time discussing this or that, but I was like in a trance every time I looked up. The clouds started looking an awful lot like baseballs floating across the sky and I thought, yup, Fred Lynn and Jim Rice were probably at that moment sending moon shots out into orbit right up there.

When we got there though, it was nice. As advertised, this was one of the best Brigham's I had been in. All brass and marble and fixtures that reminded me of that song John Kiley would pump out on the organ during rain delays, *Daisy, Daisy . . . a bicycle built for two*. Only there were three of us. That was it. There was a nice lazy after-church feel to things, and we were the only people in the place. We got our single-scoop dishes of ice cream and took them to the front window booth to look out at the square.

Which was fine for a while. Palm Sunday. Families walking along together, parents holding their three strands of dried palm respectfully, while their kids whipped each other with theirs. The atmosphere out on the small green patch at the center of the square had that unmistakable look of the true beginning of spring, with guys throwing footballs around with their jackets off, people eating food outdoors as if fresh air was an actual nutritional ingredient, and an explosion of babies all around. Not bad. Very peaceful. I was almost ready to let go of my baseball pang as the three of us sat there for a bit silently, staring out from our ice-cream world.

Until the real world stared back. All of a sudden, one of the ball tossers across the way dropped his hands as he caught sight of us in the window. The football hit him in the chest and fell to the ground in front of him. Jum McDonaugh stood there, staring dumbfounded at us, as if this could simply not be happening. Then, like a great big sewer rat he scurried over to his bike and was gone so quickly we could have imagined the whole thing.

Napoleon sat rigid as a statue.

We had not imagined it.

"Do you suppose we scared him away?" I asked.

Beverly sighed, a heavy, exhausted sigh.

Any pleasure we might have enjoyed had been choked out of our time now. Amazing that it could turn so quickly, and turn on so little.

"Should we go?" I asked. "I guess we should get going, huh?"

"Much as I hate to say it," Beverly said sadly, "it's probably best if we do."

I assumed we were all in agreement on that. It made you so mad your stomach burned, but there was no denying what we were feeling. And it would only get worse if we waited. Beverly and I put down our spoons and wiped our mouths with our big white Brigham's napkins.

Napoleon took another, very small, spoonful. He held it in his mouth for what seemed an unnecessarily long time without swallowing, and then swallowed.

He picked up another spoonful. "I am finished when I am finished," he said calmly. He wouldn't look at either one of us.

Beverly and I looked at each other.

"You're right," Beverly said. "Dead right. And I understand why you don't want to give in. I respect that. But I'm the one responsible for you being here, and I don't want to be responsible for what happens next. I don't want to see it, Napoleon."

"What if he comes back with twenty guys?" I pointed out.

He took another spoonful. Swallowed. Shrugged. "What if he comes back with twenty thousand? What is the population anyway, of Boston, Massachusetts, USA?" He took another tiny mouthful.

"If it was the whole city, I guess you'd want to fight the whole city," I said. "But it's not the whole city, so don't start that."

"Why don't you just fight each other then?" Beverly sounded disgusted.

"If you don't mind," Napoleon said, pretending to be oblivious to everything all of a sudden, "I am trying to eat."

It was the longest, slowest bowl of ice cream in history. The last eight or ten spoonfuls could have easily been done with a straw. I was getting more and more nervous, to the point where I was ready to pull Napoleon right out of the chair for his own stubborn good.

Until it occurred to me. Nothing was happening. Nothing was going to happen. It *was* possible, still, for things to get blown up worse than they were. And that's what we were doing. I was wrong. We were wrong. I was so pleased, about everyone being wrong.

"I'm getting myself a Coke," I said. "Anyone else?"

I stood to go to the counter. Confident.

And wrong again.

Jum stood up close to the window, pointing us out to Butchie.

Butchie smiled. Looked like a dog baring his teeth.

The two of them stood there for a long minute, staring at us like we were the impossible three-headed fish in the pet store window. Then they moved on away from the window and across the street.

"This is stupid," I said. "I'll go talk to him."

"Sit *down*, Richard," Napoleon said.

I sat.

"Please don't make too big a deal out of it, Napoleon,"

Beverly said. Beverly's face was making a big deal out of it, like she might cry. "He doesn't matter."

I looked outside. Jum and Butch were sitting now, in a bench at the park. Facing us. There were two more guys with them that I had never seen before. Older.

Beverly took notice too. "No, no . . ." her voice trailed away.

Then there were two more. And it looked as if they were all sitting on a wooden sofa, watching a TV that was the Brigham's window.

"They're just like dogs," Beverly said. "Territorial. Brainless."

"And what," I said, "they don't like other dogs in their yard? And anyway, I thought this wasn't even their yard."

"Apparently their yard is getting larger," Napoleon said.

We all stared out for a few seconds, waiting for whatever. But it was waiting for us.

"I am so sorry about this," Beverly said.

Napoleon stood up, wiped his mouth neatly at the corners with his napkin as he continued staring out across the way. Even now, he still had his manners. I thought of him and his father together in Pier 4, so graceful, so foreign, so many million miles away from here and now.

I could not ever remember actually wanting to fight anybody before. Before this moment.

"You want to go fight?" I asked.

"Don't be stupid," Beverly said to me.

Napoleon pulled his lips tight. His eyes went narrow

as he looked out there, and he began lightly, rhythmically tapping the table with the meaty part of his fist.

"Yes, I want to fight," he said.

I thought Beverly was going to scream, or cry, or attack Napoleon herself.

"If you do," she said, pointing a finger at him, "if you do . . ." She stalled, to collect herself. "*They* are animals. What's *your* excuse?"

Napoleon looked out the window at the faces in the park. They were hardening as we spoke, freezing and whitening, into hateful stony statues. Then he looked at Beverly, then at me, before finally nodding at Beverly.

"I have never struck anyone before," he said to her.

"I believe you," she said.

"I could do it now, however."

"I believe you."

Napoleon stood then, and with smooth, slow, graceful motions, took his napkin, wiped the corners of his mouth. He refolded the napkin, placed it beside his plate as neatly as he found it. He put on his coat.

"This is a sad place," he said.

The three of us walked out to the sidewalk, looked at the bunch of them for a minute, then headed toward the bus stop.

"There ya go," Butch called, to the sound of supporting laughter. "Good boy. Smart boy. Don't get lost again now. Who knows what could happen to a lost boy in the big city?"

I tipped a glance toward Napoleon. The muscles in his temples were bunching and bunching and bunching.

"They're all talk," Beverly said. "They would never really *do* anything."

"Was that not anything?" he said. He sounded exhausted.

I thought then, I would be exhausted all the time if I was Napoleon Charlie Ellis.

It's exhausting enough just being with him.

A
HIGHER
CALLING

As promised, Mr. Connolly was at the school on Monday. He was making the rounds of the classes starting with first grade, listening to every voice in the school in his search for talent. Apparently this was Mr. Connolly's full-time job, going around to all the schools in the Archdiocese and recruiting for the choir school. We could hear the squeaky little voices of the lower grades, as they sang to the piano in the basement room that was directly below Sister Jacqueline's homeroom. Sister kept smiling sweetly at every warbling, every screech. But every minute or so she would look back toward Napoleon Charlie Ellis and give a knowing nod. As if it was all just a formality, and we all knew why Connolly was really here. Which, this being a kind of intimate little school, I suppose we did.

Some of us did, anyway. Some of us didn't particularly care.

"Hey," Butchie said, apparently to me and Napoleon

both. "What's the deal? The Judge decide all the Brigham'ses in the city need to be desegregated now?"

The two of us wheeled around to face him.

"I will not waste my time on this ignorance of yours," Napoleon said, then turned right in his seat again.

Which left me facing Butch. "See what I mean," he said to me, pointing a finger straight at Napoleon's back. "Thinks he's too good to waste his time on the likes of me."

I nodded. Finally, I did see.

"He is," I said. "So am I."

"Oooh," Butchie said with a cheesy fake smile on his face. "I been waitin' for this. Finally you ain't white trash anymore?"

"Nope." I did my best imitation of the Ellis composure I had seen so much of. I looked at the back of my hand. "Still white. Just ain't *trash*."

"In your dreams, Riley," he said, but it didn't matter. As far as I was concerned the conversation was already over.

Now Napoleon and I were both facing front. For a second.

I tipped a look his way. "All right."

He didn't look back. "All right?"

"All right, you were maybe right."

He looked at me now, just as I looked away.

"About time," he said, then went back to his book.

He was not about to cut me any slack, give me any

credit, or call off his dogs for one single minute. He was determined to be miserable no matter what. There was a lot of tough stuff to admire about Napoleon, but then he could turn around and drive you nuts with that very same stuff. Well, now I wasn't going to give in all the way, either.

"You were right about *him*." I said. "*Not* about everybody everywhere."

He just kept to his book.

At eleven that morning we were all gathered around the piano. All the boys in my class anyway. They divided us by gender as well as age, I guess in an effort to group all voices approximately according to similar sound. They had that wrong.

"Stop, stop, stop, wait a minute," Mr. Connolly said after grimacing through the first six notes of the C scale with all of us as a group. "You," he said to me. "Is that you, making that . . . sound?"

"'Fraid so," I said. I didn't mind. Expected it, really.

"I'm sorry, son, but would you mind terribly . . . not singing?"

"Not terribly," I said, while most of my classmates laughed.

Which, a little less conspicuously, was how the process went. One by one, Connolly would isolate a singer from the group, ask him to hit a note or two, then weed that guy out.

Until in the end there was one lone voice. And that

voice was so strong and clear, and surprisingly high—he hit a note like that little whistle piping an admiral aboard ship, and held it a long time—that everyone in the room just stood there gawking silently. We did a lot of gawking in this group, but usually not silently.

I had so much time, during the miracle of that long note, that I traveled, through January, and February, through the snow and ice and muck and arguments and symphony and Pier 4 and above all, across baseball fields, snowy ones and arid rock-frost ones and asphalt ones and finally fantastic grassy springtime ones, hitting and pitching and fielding and coaching and talking and even, unbelievably, learning.

Napoleon's one unbelievable otherworldly note ran through me.

When he had finally let go, Mr. Connolly went practically mental with clapping, and the rest of the class followed. I thought Connolly was going to cry.

"That was . . . that was . . ." With the words not coming, Mr. Connolly went back to the hand-shaking thing. He really was a fan by now.

I had to slap my man on the back. I didn't know if this was what you did to singing stars, but I knew it was what you did to athletes who scored. And that's what this felt like.

"You didn't even sound human, man. That was great. Does everybody in Dominica sound like that?"

"No," he said, looking down, shaking his head. Then he looked up at me, shaking his head again.

"What?" I asked. I couldn't believe the million ways it

was possible for my mouth to open and his head to shake. I should have stuck to the language I knew and slapped his back a few more times.

Which was what I did. It was a spasm, but the right spasm, as he started laughing . . . along with shaking his head.

For the most part, Napoleon looked a little embarrassed by the whole thing. Which must have made it a whole lot harder for him when Sister Jacqueline stood side by side with Mr. Connolly at the head of the class at the end of the day to make the big announcement.

". . . and this is such an honor, such a banner day for St. Colmcille's, as we have never placed one of our students with the prestigious and nationally famous Archdiocese Choir School in all the years they have been testing us. And for our Napoleon to be offered a full scholarship . . ."

When the time came, I clapped as hard as anyone. I felt proud, like somewhere in there I had something to do with Napoleon's achievement. I was the one who took him under my wing, after all.

And besides, it wasn't as if he was actually going to go. I clapped harder as I thought that. And harder and harder, and my hands turned red, and all thoughts melted harmlessly away.

He was out of school again the next day. Hurt himself singing, I figured. It was a pretty high note he hit after all. Or maybe he was just letting this thing die down since he was obviously not a limelight kind of a guy.

At lunch I got in the game. Stickball. And I was a monster. I hit whatever was thrown at me. First pitch every time. It was as if I couldn't even wait for the ball to reach me, I was so prepared, so ready, so *ahead* of the game I was in.

He did that for me. All these guys I had been playing with before, they were just a step slower and a thought behind now. Napoleon's pitching all these weeks, faster and nastier than anything I had faced before, improved me. Even without him here at this moment, we were still operating as one machine, because of all that we had done together. I could not wait for youth league season to start. Napoleon and I were going to eat that league up.

The Gold Dust Twins. Just rolling the words through my head raised bumps on my skin higher than the pimples on the pimple ball.

But.

But.

"So what are you gonna *do* now?" Quin asked. He had his hand on his cheek and his head tilted like this was really worrying him. He was trying anything to crack my concentration before pitching to me.

"What are you talking about?" I asked.

"Without your *shadow*."

Did I imagine it? Or did he really lean on that word? "Shadow." No. No, I had to stop now. I was getting as bad as . . .

"Shut up. He's nobody's shadow."

"Whatever. But you'll be back to being one of us, now that he's gone."

"He's not gone. Jeez, a guy stays out one day and you make a big . . . there ain't no way he's gonna go there."

"Fool. He ain't sick. He's over touring that weenie choir school right now. Sister said so."

"You don't know anything. Shut up and throw me the ball."

Quin smiled. Figured he had done what he set out to do, which was rattle me. Fine. That's the game. Nothing more than the game.

The ball came, out of the sky from that big ol' swooping windup of his. Zinging out over the outside edge of the plate.

And smack, I hit it.

And *smack*. The ball bounced right off Quin's forehead and went high up in the air.

Manny caught it when it finally came down, and I was out. Fine with me.

I went down to the field that day with Manny and Glen, Quin, Arthur Brown, and Arthur's brother Gary. It was just too much like spring for people to resist anymore. We took turns pitching and catching, shagging flies, and fielding grounders. This was it now, the transition stage from mechanical-type drills to actual baseball-game activity, and it got my adrenaline pumping. I ran around all that afternoon like a headless haunted ballplayer, chasing every ball, retrieving every foul, catching, throwing, just doing whatever necessary to make myself work, and breathe hard. Breathing *baseball* was what I was doing. The scent had changed already, from mud and frost to mud and grass.

But.

But.

I needed something different than I needed last year or the year before.

And after an hour of this, he appeared. Walking up over the hill that led to the field, I recognized Napoleon Charlie Ellis's rigid upright stride from well off. I walked to meet him partway, and when I reached him on the left-field sideline, he looked serious. He smiled, but it wasn't an easy smile.

Maybe it was the clothes.

"Why would you wear your school stuff to baseball, man? In fact, why would you wear your school clothes at all, since you didn't go to school?"

"I went to the choir school today," he said evenly. "And I have not been home to change yet."

"Oh," I said, and let that hang there. I sort of wanted him to do the talking. He owed me an explanation, after all. Going to that place without even telling me. He owed me an explanation.

"You don't owe me any explanation," I said finally, coolly.

"It is a very nice place," he said.

He was doing the talking, but I had to bring him along. Had to get him to say what I wanted before he made the mistake of saying what I didn't want.

"You gonna play in those clothes?"

"I think I won't play today."

"What?" I said. I looked up at the perfect baseball sky, the perfect baseball day, then at Napoleon. He knew what I meant.

"Come on, will ya?" Manny called from the field. "It's your ups, Richard. You wanna hit, or no?"

"So what are you doing here?" I asked.

This time he smiled for real. He drew two tickets out of his pocket. For the Red Sox' first Saturday home game of the season, against the Oakland A's. First-base line. Right behind the coach's box.

My mouth hung open.

"They were a gift," Napoleon said. "It appears these people *really* want me to attend their school."

"For this, *I'll* go to their corny music school," I said, still staring at the tickets.

"Actually I believe the deal is, they said I could give you one if you promised *not* to ever sing again."

"Deal," I said, snatching the ticket away.

But as soon as I did, I felt as if I'd traded something that I didn't want to trade. There was now officially no such thing as a purely good thing.

Napoleon nodded. "So go back to your game now. I

just wanted to tell you that." He started walking away.

"There's still time," I said. "You could change and come back."

I was looking at his back, then to the field, almost *placing* him there in the game with my eyes.

"I am just too tired," he said. I watched his back as he walked. Looked like he was telling the truth.

And sounded like he knew what he was doing.

"So they really want you bad, huh?" I asked.

"Yes they do," he answered. "It is a nice feeling, actually."

I turned back toward the field, where somebody was trying to take my turn at bat. "Ya, I guess," I said.

GOLD
DUST

Fenway is considered a small park. One of the smallest in the major league. A bandbox, they call it.

But Fenway was enormous to me. In every way. When you approached from the outside on Jersey Street on a game day, the size of everything was enough to blow you right over. The crowds of people could crush you, moving the way they do more in circles than in a straight line toward the entrances. The sausage sellers, themselves mostly pretty giant guys, had big voices on them that went over and through even the wildest fans. We stood there for a couple of minutes that day, me and Napoleon, and even though there was that constant fear that the movement of people could crush us or, at the very least, bounce us right out onto the Mass Turnpike if we weren't lucky, we had to stop and stare.

The exposed green girders that held up the stands all around were about the most massive hunks of steel I had ever seen. There were loads of taller buildings around, especially the Prudential and the Hancock towers, which we could see just as well if we decided to turn a few degrees one way. But for my money there was nothing this *big* anywhere in the whole city. Fenway made a constant rumble and roar on a game day, and even seemed to be laughing, in a way a giant would laugh. It was scary, in a way. But a thrilling scare.

"I have not seen anything like this," Napoleon said, as bigger people rushed past, bumping me into Napoleon, and him into me. "Carnival, in Trinidad, is a spectacle and very exciting. But *that*," he pointed up at the highest bit of the grandstand and then at the huge mouth of the entrance dead ahead of us, "that is like a monster that swallows people and then hollers for more."

I was pleased. There was the thing, right there, that kept us going. Whatever little things went wrong and whatever little signs came up that we were just too different . . . *bam*, he would come up with the goods and remind me that we were not that far apart at all, when you dug underneath and got to what was really in there. That was why I could keep knowing things would work out right.

Was the place magic, or what?

"So," I said, "you want to let it swallow *us*?"

"Let's."

In we went, with the crush of people narrowing and narrowing through the gate until it felt like we would be squeezed through the eye of a needle eventually. But we got through, and ran up the concrete ramp that delivered us, like some kind of fantastic trick, into the inside/outside of Fenway Park.

The grass that spilled wide and far in front of us was the greenest grass you would ever see. And it led, like a carpet, out and out to the walls of the outfield, telling us when it got there just how far it had traveled. Painted in yellow on each bit of wall, three hundred and fifteen feet to the foul pole in right, four hundred and five to dead center, and, famously, a mere two hundred seventy-nine feet down the line in left. You would think almost anybody could hit a ball out of the park in Fenway's left field. Except that at the end of the line was the Green Monster—a piece of wall that went up, and up and up, thirty feet up, and topped by the nets to catch balls that actually did clear it and keep them from konking heads out there on the street. And the old mechanical scoreboard was built right into that wall, with little squirrelly people inside working to post all the results from Fenway and every other game in the country.

It was impossible that anybody, anybody in the world, could stand here and not be swept totally away by it. That's what I thought then, and I was sure Napoleon Charlie Ellis was thinking the same thing. I was dead certain of it.

"So they want you bad over there at that singing school," I said, still looking off. "How soon?"

"Whenever. I can go next week, if I like. Though next September is probably what they are thinking about."

That was a test. It was like Napoleon was a turkey in the oven and I had just poked him with a fork to see if he was done. If he was done, he would have said, Ah, what singing school. Why would I leave all this for some dumb old singing school? He would have said, I'm sticking with you, twin. He would have said, This is the dream, right here, us at Fenway Park, not warbling away in some church choir someplace.

He was not done yet. Not quite ready. But he would be soon. He had to be. Nothing else made sense.

Fenway Park, though, had to do the work. The Red Sox would do the work, better than anything I could say. "Hmm," was all I did say. Then I let myself drift away from that again.

You could not avoid the smell of grass, and popcorn, and hot dogs, even if you held your nose. You could not avoid the music of John Kiley's organ if you blocked your ears, because it would come up from the floor and travel through your legs and your whole body to reach your brain. And when Sherm Feller the announcer, with that voice so much deeper and thicker than any human sound I ever heard anywhere else, announced that it was time for us to stand for the national anthem, Napoleon and I scrambled, realizing that we had once again been caught flatfooted and staring, like a couple of yokels up to the big city for the day. This was a new experience for

Napoleon, but for me there was no excuse.

When we were finally seated, it was a thrill all over again. I had never had seats this good before.

"Can you believe how close we are to the players?" I said in his ear. "Look how white their uniforms are."

"That is what cricket players look like all the time," he said. "As if they do their laundry every time they leave the playing field. Actually I prefer Oakland's uniforms."

"Cripes," I said. The A's, because they had a nutty owner named Charlie O. Finley, who brought his pet donkey for a mascot and paid his players to wear waxed 1890s mustaches, wore the most bizarre outfits in the game. Dark green shirts and yellow hats. It was just crazy.

"And I like their mustaches," Napoleon added.

I couldn't help it. Maybe this was one of those moments Beverly likes to point out, where my baseball-mania is over the top and I lose perspective. But I was getting bothered. By the way Napoleon was looking at the A's, and the way he was looking at The Game. The uniforms and facial hair were not the point. In fact, they were distracting from the point.

Baseball people didn't love Charlie O. Finley and his quirks. Baseball people loved *baseball*.

And Boston people loved the Red Sox. Not the A's.

But all this stuff fell gradually away once the game started. I wouldn't really have noticed whether they were playing at Fenway, or Wrigley in Chicago with its ivy-covered outfield wall, or Kansas City with its fountain just beyond the fence in center. Luis Tiant was pitching, and the A's—Billy North and Joe Rudi and Reggie Jackson and Sal Bando—were hitting.

Tiant was amazing. He was famous for his delivery, which had him spin completely around so that he was facing center field in the middle of his windup before coming in after the hitter. He was so good, and so fascinating to watch, that he was working on his third hitter when I was nudged by Napoleon and looked up. He had left and come back with two hot dogs and two Cokes.

"Wow, thanks," I said.

He gestured toward Tiant. "He is really funny, the way he does that."

I knew he bought me a hot dog and everything, but this was serious.

"He's not funny. He's a genius."

"Oh. Sorry."

We went back to watching, and Tiant finished off the side.

"This is when the good stuff starts," I said, munching hot dogs with Napoleon. "The Sox hitters. Yaz and Burleson and Dwight Evans, and, of course . . ."

I was pretty obvious with my cue, but I wanted to be sure he got it.

"Right," Napoleon said. "The . . . Gold Dust Twins."

There was a slight hitch in there. Like the words didn't quite leap to mind. Those words should have been leaping to mind.

I patted him on the back. He patted me on the back. I saw I had gotten mustard on his back, and I coolly took my napkin and dabbed at it without telling him. When he started doing the same move, we both laughed.

"All right," I said when the game started up again.

Catfish Hunter was pitching for Oakland, which was good and bad. Good, because we got to see one of the all-time great pitchers. Bad because he would probably strike a lot of guys out, which means not a lot of hits, which can be a bummer. Not to mention he could win by doing that.

"Catfish," Napoleon said. "That is a colorful nick-name. Why is he called Catfish?"

I looked at him for a second. I started to talk, restarted. I was suddenly embarrassed, as if somehow this reflected badly on me. "Finley, the owner, gave it to him. Made it up out of nowhere, because he thought it sounded good."

Napoleon nodded, but his face told it all. He smiled kindly on me like I was responsible and he felt bad for me.

I had known that story for a long time. It never mattered to me before. Now telling it to Napoleon made me hear how stupid it was. Why did I have to hear that? Why did I even have to think about that?

By the time I had taken the last sip of my drink, the great pitcher with the awful nickname had easily retired the first three Red Sox he had faced. The Twins would have to wait.

During the break I turned to make conversation with

Napoleon, but he was staring off. I followed his line of vision out to the big neon Citgo sign outside the park, stretching up from the top of a building in Kenmore Square. It was this busy, moving, pulsating triangle of light that was so central to any Sox television broadcast, you would think the thing was sitting in the middle of the field.

"I like that sign," Napoleon said. He looked half asleep.

"That old thing?" I asked. "I guess it's all right. I personally think right-handed batters try too hard to jerk a ball into that sign. But I guess it looks okay."

"My father works right over there," he said, indicating the square, where Boston University was spread all up and down Commonwealth Avenue.

I hadn't thought about this before, but as soon as he mentioned it, I felt like asking. "Ya," I said, "about that. You think he'll work there for a long time? Like, you'll stay?"

Napoleon shrugged. "This position may be long-term," he said, but without a lot of feeling. "No problem."

The players were filing back onto the field, but I was not ready for them yet.

"What does that mean, no problem?"

"It means, I don't mind. I have moved before. I can move again."

No problem. He didn't mind. No problem.

Maybe I was mistaken. All the way through. Maybe all

those times I thought Napoleon just wasn't understanding one thing or another I had it all backward. Maybe when I thought he was always cool, always trying to keep himself under control and all, maybe he wasn't trying at all.

Maybe . . . maybe there was nothing to control in the first place. Maybe there was nothing there. Maybe he didn't feel anything in the same way I felt it.

Maybe he didn't care.

"From here? You wouldn't mind leaving?"

I had to check. I somehow figured that by rewording it, he would see it more as I would.

"No, I wouldn't mind, I guess," he said, turning his attention to the field.

"Oh," I said. Turning mine.

"Did you say *ow*?" he asked.

"'Course not," I said. "I said *oh*." Stupid thing to ask a guy. Ow means you're hurt. Oh means . . . you really don't care.

Jim Rice. I nudged Napoleon. He nodded. He had a power, Rice did, that was a lot more noticeable in person than on TV. Even though he was mighty powerful on TV. The crowd gave him a loud cheer, very excited. Very impressive treatment for a rookie. A knowledgeable crowd.

And Rice looked anxious to unleash his power for them. But Catfish wasn't all about power, and he was a crafty vet to Rice's eager rookie. It took exactly three pitches for him to send the first Twin back to the dugout. But it was a very powerful strikeout.

And then it was Lynn. And when Lynn came up, something happened. Half the crowd stood. A semi-standing ovation. The sound was thunderous, and John Kiley helped it along with some big fat organ chords he must have been playing with his feet. I stood. It was impossible to resist. Fred Lynn was the thing, the man, what we had been waiting for in Boston since the Sox' last World Series victory in 1918.

Napoleon Charlie Ellis sat.

Three pitches later, we were all sitting again. Including Fred Lynn.

"Hunter pitched him really tough," I said, sort of apologizing for my man. "How come you weren't up on your feet?"

"These people love Fred Lynn," he said. Not an answer.

"What's not to love?" I said. "It's okay to stand up when you get excited, you know."

"He struck out."

"Happens to the best of them sometimes."

"So it does," he said.

It went about like that for most of the game, a classic pitcher's duel. Which is a great thing if you are a baseball purist. But it's deadly if you are trying to introduce a newcomer. Napoleon's attention was constantly wandering, and once it hit him how expensive it was to kill time at Fenway by snacking, that too lost its attraction. He was having much less of a fine time than I thought he would.

You could feel it, in the space between us. He was drifting away.

We were standing for the seventh-inning stretch.

"Is the game over?" he asked. He did not sound disappointed.

"No. This is just the point where they figure you need to loosen up a bit."

"Oh," he said.

"So what do you think, Napoleon?" I asked.

They say that baseball is a fine art, an acquired taste for the newcomer. One that takes time to learn to appreciate, and maybe I should have prepared Napoleon better. Because it must have been impatience that made him come out with the answer he did.

"I think maybe it is the boredom element which keeps black people from coming here."

I did not even know where to begin to respond to that. I opened my mouth, but nothing came out. So I considered the angles, considered the approach, considered Napoleon's point of view, considered the sport, the park, the teams, considered Catfish Hunter's unfortunately masterful day. And still nothing came out.

So I looked. Followed again Napoleon's line of vision, up our side of the stands, into the right-field bleachers, across sun-bleached center field, over to the third base line, behind home plate, up into the grandstands, down into the boxes, rounding the final turn like a runner trying to score, and finally back, all the way up to us, up to where

I met Napoleon Charlie Ellis's face right up in mine.

"Is it always like that?" he asked.

I waited. We sat down again as the stretch ended. I started watching the game, even though the game had not yet started back up.

"I said, is it always like that here, Richard? It is just a question."

"The answer is, I don't know, Napoleon." It was the absolute truth. I had no idea. Had never noticed. Had never checked. "I was always watching the game," I said. I shrugged. "I'm sorry."

I had never said anything like that before. There was never any reason to apologize for baseball. And truth was, I didn't feel the need to apologize now. It just seemed like the right thing to say.

I bought the next round of Cokes. The game dragged on. The pitchers continued to be great. The hitters continued to be not. Jim Rice didn't get a hit all day. Neither did Fred Lynn, although he walked once and then got picked off trying to steal second. He's not speedy. He's quick. He had to remember that. He got a nice ovation for the attempt, though.

"They clap for Fred Lynn even when he appears to have done something foolish," Napoleon said.

A small growl came out of me. "They were applauding the *effort*, Napoleon, the hustle." He was *refusing* to understand things. I was sure of it now.

"And when he struck out, that took great effort?"

"Maybe," I said.

"He struck out, the same as Jim Rice."

"Like I told you, it happens—"

"But the people clapped madly for Mr. Lynn anyway. Not so much for Mr. Rice." Napoleon had by now given up any pose of being casual with his questions. It became interrogation. "What does that mean, Richard?"

You know the moment. Like when an important paper comes back with a large F on it. When your father tells you he has searched everywhere but it seems the dog just won't be coming back. Or there's a phone call and you're the only one home, and the person on the other end is sorry but there has been an accident. . . .

And you don't get to digest it slowly over time because it is a punch, hard in the stomach.

"No, Napoleon," I said. "Stop. You're not going to do your *thing*. Please. Not now. Not to *this*." I pointed at the field, Joe Mooney's perfectly groomed field, that was perfectly groomed for *us*, to enjoy all spring and summer and right through to the World Series in October when Napoleon and I could be right back here again, watching history.

"Did you know," Napoleon said calmly, like a professor, "that there is a country club in Winter Haven, Florida, where the Red Sox golf during spring training? All the players get complimentary membership cards when they arrive. Except the black players. I read that in the newspaper. Did you know that?"

I was gripping the arms of my seat. My stomach was

jumping. I threw my head back and stared straight up. "I told you not to go reading the papers. I told you that would only—"

"Did I tell you that my father was discussing Lynn and Rice with another man at the university and when my father suggested that Lynn was possibly not the better player the other man said, 'Oh, you must be one of them Ricists.' He thought that was funny. A joke."

I said nothing. Napoleon could talk all he wanted to. He could pile one fact on top of another on top of another on top of my body and then he could go on and kick that body as hard and as many times as he liked, because he had already done his worst.

To me.

Something in him, I guessed, had to do this but I was never, ever, *never* going to understand it. Newspapers and universities and country clubs and all the rest are just poison. They don't do anybody any good. What I had, what I thought *we* had, was better than all that. It was better, and it was great, and I really really really loved it because of what it was all by itself, inside itself.

Napoleon didn't understand, after all.

The game ended quietly. When the sun starts going down in the late innings of the early season, it gets very cold very quickly at Fenway Park. You can almost feel people wishing the game to end. The hitters start looking stiffer, and the guys out in the field keep blowing on their hands to thaw them.

The A's won 2–0. It was a fine game if you appreciated

the sport, a waste of time if you did not. It was quiet enough on the way out that you could have a normal-level conversation and be heard.

"Why do you have to keep doing this to me?" I said to Napoleon, who was walking ahead of me at about the middle of the line of 32,149 pale cold Bostonians. "It's *baseball*. Man, it's *baseball*. Why do you have to be like that?"

I didn't expect an answer. But maybe an apology. He took something away, he owed me something back.

I was way off, and I should have known.

"Because I have to," he said.

He sounded sad. But it wasn't an apology.

I
SWEAR

I swear I didn't mean it.

I had picked my team, like usual, put Napoleon on it, like usual.

Then traded myself. Switched teams with Manny just as the game was to start.

I wanted to pitch. To him.

I had by that time thrown probably ten thousand pitches to Napoleon Charlie Ellis, and never once came seriously close to hitting him. Which made this even worse. Because he just stood there, like a big dumb sense-less defenseless sitting cow when the ball—we were using a hard orange hockey ball that day as we edged closer to real baseballs—came in, started low and rose, rose, came inside, inside. . . .

That's the game. That's my job. If I had never in all that time brushed Napoleon Charlie Ellis back with a pitch, then that was my mistake. I should have been preparing him better.

But it was only a brushback. I was just playing the game.

He never flinched. Because he never would have expected it. Not from me.

The ball hit Napoleon square in the mouth. It sort of sank into him, then just died there, falling at his feet. He blinked, raised his hand to his mouth, then looked at the little bit of blood that had seeped from the small split in his lower lip. He looked blankly at me.

He was in shock.

I was in shock. I would never, ever have done that on purpose.

Would I?

The game went quiet. I had already seen Sister come out into the yard with her bell, so this was when we should have been at our noisiest. There were a couple of low murmers behind me, the *woooo* kind that guys make when they are trying to whip something small into something bigger.

I took a few steps toward Napoleon. "Sorry," I said. My voice was dead, though. It didn't sound good enough, but good enough just wouldn't come. "It got away from me."

He nodded. He was nothing if not leather-tough. He reached down and picked up the ball and threw it back to me. We didn't do walks around here.

Napoleon got back into his crouch. And I got back into my windup.

And did it again.

It traveled just about the exact same line, low-to-high, bearing in. But this time he reacted at the last second, spun away from the pitch, and took it in the back.

And then he came my way.

He was right. He should have come.

But it *was* an accident. A freak. I'd lost the handle.

None of that mattered.

I met him halfway, ready, hands up. We grabbed each other, looked into each other's faces. Don't know what mine was showing, but Napoleon's was a combination of teeth-gritting anger and drippy-eyed sadness. I was dying to say I was sorry, but it was just not coming out of me. I don't know if he was waiting for that or not, but we were taking too much time deciding to hurt each other.

I could hear the low buzz out there, in that way you can hear those things even they don't sound like actual voices that belong to anybody. "Hit him," they said, "hit him." I agreed with them. Hit me, I was thinking. Hit me.

Until the buzz actually cleared, and got specific. "Kill him, Richard," was what I heard. "Mess him up."

What? Kill him, *Richard*?

The bell started clanging. I held on to the collar of his shirt. Napoleon ran out of patience. Grabbing me tighter and tighter around my collar, pushing his thumbs into my throat, he was beginning to choke me. He gritted his teeth. A small, high moan came out of him.

And then Napoleon Charlie Ellis did what he had spent all his time since I'd known him—maybe all his life—trying not to do. He broke.

He cried.

Then he dumped me. Pulled as tight as possible around my neck, bounced me hard down onto the pavement. His glasses hit the ground at the same time I did. I looked down at them, then up at him.

He was in perfect position. I was there, my head was there, just waiting to be teed off.

He leaned toward me, scooped up his glasses, and walked toward the ringing bell.

I sat on the ground for another minute. Watched Napoleon walk with a sort of force field around him, nobody coming within ten feet of him.

Somebody slapped me on the shoulder on his way past. Then somebody else did. Then three or four more. What for? Idiots, *I* was the bad guy. I slapped away one more hand. I couldn't even bear to raise my head and look.

Then there was a hand in my face. Butchie, offering me a hand up. "Another nasty interracial incident in a Boston school," he said slyly, shaking his head. "Is no place safe anymore?" He laughed.

It had come to that. I had made Butch happy.

"Get away from me, before I puke on both of us," I said, getting up on my own.

• • •

The next morning, even before the first bell rang, I sat next to Napoleon's empty seat and waited, waited for what I already sort of knew. If he had shown up . . . I don't know what I would have done if he had shown up. Probably nothing.

Manny took Napoleon's seat. "Wanna get up a game this afternoon?"

"Ya," I said automatically, not much thinking who I was talking to.

"So," Manny said casually, looking around. "He's gone."

There was really no need to answer. And suddenly the idea of talking made me very tired.

"Hey, you tried," he said. "I don't even know why. He didn't want to know nobody. He didn't belong here. He's better off with all the singers and weirdos at that other place."

I was staring at him hard. Manny. I could usually find something helpful in there, in Manny's open face. "You think?" I said.

"I know it. Look, I know about getting along. You want to get along you at least meet people halfway. He wasn't meeting nobody noplace. He didn't want to get along."

I thought about that, whether I thought it was true. Thought about if I could even tell *what* was true about Napoleon.

"Ya, maybe," I said. "Maybe he just didn't want to try.

Or maybe he really was the most negative guy ever. Or maybe everything and everybody was just as bad as he said."

Manny started leaning away from me. "Okay, so you don't want to talk about it."

"Something you want to share with the rest of the class, Richard and Manuel?" Sister Jacqueline said dramatically.

"No, Sister," we moaned together.

By the walk home I was feeling strangely pumped full of energy. I had received invitations to play ball from so many different people that a full five-on-five home-run derby was going to be possible down at the field that afternoon. That alone was reason for cheer, and gradually as the day wore on I was feeling less tired.

So what if I was walking alone? That was what I had always done, before.

Right. He should have just left me alone in the first place. I was fine before he got here. Finer, even. I was great before he got here. I would be great again.

I felt the tap on my shoulder. "Walk me to my stop?"

I nodded.

"He's gone," she said after a few steps.

"Why does everybody keep saying that?"

"Touchy."

"Hey, Beverly, I tried to be his friend, but he saw something wrong with everything. I even had this idea, that we would be the Gold Dust Twins, in baseball, like Rice and Lynn, together all the way. Stupid. What a stupid dream. Such a *kid*'s dream."

"It was a sweet dream," Beverly said. Then waited.

"It just wasn't *his* dream," she said.

"It could have been."

"No. . . ."

"Yes it could. He was just so difficult all the time."

"Did you ever wonder, Richard, what Napoleon's dreams are? Did you ever even ask him?"

"Isn't this your stop?" I growled. We'd come to a street-cleaning sign.

"How come you never knew about his singing after all that time?"

I didn't like the question she asked. So I just answered one she didn't. "My dream was big enough for both of us," I said. I could hear how childish I sounded, but I could not stop.

"I was doing fine before he showed up. Before all of you showed up. It was so much easier before . . . everything was just great."

This time we had reached her stop. The bus was approaching.

"He had no *right*," I snapped.

Beverly looked at me calmly, kindly, as if she just didn't believe me, whatever I was saying, and wouldn't react.

"I'm going to be seeing him this afternoon," she said. "You want to come?"

As quickly as I could, I shook my head, hard. "I have a game to play," I said.

"You want me to tell him anything?"

The bus door opened. The driver did not look like he'd wait.

"You can't tell that guy anything," I said, and turned to go before she did.

I walked on. The bus doors shut. The engine wheezed into gear.

I started running.

I ran down the sidewalk, jogging at first, then trotting, then running hard down the line, running, running, legging it out, until the bus caught up to me. I veered out into the street, waved him down. He stopped. They don't do that a lot in Boston. I must have looked desperate.

I walked halfway to the back, swaying side-to-side, holding seat backs for balance, until I tumbled into the seat next to her.

Beverly looked at me, waiting.

"Tell him I'm sorry. Tell him I'm sorry and good luck. Tell him I hope he's great. Tell him I know he's going to be great.

"Tell him that," I said, hopping up and heading for the exit.

She nodded.

I got off at the next stop. I could feel myself pounding down the sidewalk. I saw the bus pass me again out of the corner of my eye. I was pumped now, and more so with every step. I could feel the old lightness and energy kind of surging back up through me, and I knew I was full of it this afternoon, full of pure baseball, all baseball, nothing but baseball.

I was going to be great.